THE DEALERS' YARD
And Other Stories

THE DEALERS' YARD

• And Other Stories •

Sharon Sheehe Stark

WILLIAM MORROW and COMPANY, INC.
New York

To Joseph and Lillian Sheehe

Acknowledgments

For every kind of encouragement, assistance, service, and mercy, I am individually and deeply grateful to the following crassly unclassified crew:

Howard N. Stark, Julie and Tim Stark. Margaret Metz, typist-cryptographer. Richard Barsotti, Kathy Moser, Vincent Balitas, Barb Crooker. Harry Humes, Jack Lindeman, Bruce Hunsberger. My dear friend and fellow seeker Barbara Reisner. Lottie Robins, Ernest Faust. Sue Hoffman and Brian Sheehe. Robert Pack, Carol Knauss, and Diane Lefer. Mary C. Yuhas, of the forbidden broomstraw. Sister Mary Giles, S.C., Sister M. Paul, O.S.M., Wm. C. Millihizer. The Lehigh Valley chapter of the FWG, circa 1980.

For her keen insights and tender methods I am particularly indebted to my friend and editor, Maria Guarnaschelli.

Very special thanks to Bryan Sheehy, of Templetouhy and Granville Center. T. H. Sheehe, who wants to be in my book and shall be, by God. And to my beloved grandmother, Juliana Kukovitz, for the gift of joy, the fire under all my words.

Contents

His Color

Even his effects were few and inconspicuous. I remember two pairs of shoes, a styptic stick, a high-school medal for the low hurdles, a bottle of Serutan. We lived in a big house, but I have the impression of my father's having conserved the space he occupied, slipping in sideways like a bookmark: the rest of us so large and unstoppable. He moved quietly through those rooms, ate little, never snored. We took his money, his closet space, his Pendleton shirt, the city chicken from his plate. He was proud of his civil service job and proud of us. He loved every car he ever owned. When he'd say, "One of these days I'm going to lower the boom," we answered him with playful cowering and hugs that threw him radically off-balance.

In his first family he was seventh of fifteen. A twenties portrait shows them in Sunday best spread fanlike across the veranda, each body rotated slightly toward the paterfamilias. My father is between six and eight, a slender lad wedged in a biological wrinkle: Only a tuft of hair shows, a round knob of shoulder, and lower down you see a fist gripping the top edge of a vaguely shield-shaped thing that upon closer inspection turns out to have a cross-knotted tail. It's a kite. In so formal a grouping, a kite seems simultaneously prankish and mystical. The kite restores this family to its arguments and animations, the minutes just before, for instance, a boy called from the meadow, the primpings and pinnings and shuffling fuss, a chaos thick enough to camouflage the small trespass of a kid's kite. The kite blossoms whole welts of life and sky around the moment in which these shining Irish faces are fixed forever.

There were the Blue Eyes and the Brown Eyes, so I've been told, and my father's mother, with her sharp dark gaze, loved the brown-eyed babes the best. My father's father stands with his chin tipped out, self-made and self-absorbed, handsome in a white suit, audacious, entitled eyes; he had The Gift, I remember, and when he spoke it was as if by heavenly mandate, his words as meaningless and wonderful as wind chimes.

Today, a half-century later, my father's voice sings no such music through my bones. "Your brother's coming," he says flatly, over the phone. "Yep, bringing them all, Dee, the kids . . ."

"Hey!" I say. "We haven't all been together—it must be nine, ten years." The silence says the rest: We might never be again.

"Yeah, well," he says, uncomfortable. "The plane tickets alone . . ." His boasts are always encumbered by the accents of complaint. "Darn kid spends money like it's going out of water—out of business. I mean out of . . ."

"Style?" I offer.

"Yep, that's what I said—style." He speaks the way he dresses. Whatever shirt is handiest. Whatever word.

"Look, why doesn't everyone come down here? Bud,

12

Patsy, everybody. I've got lots of room, the pool for the kids."

"No!"

"No?" Coming from him the word is almost a non-sense syllable.

"I'm staying right where I am! *I'm* head of this family. The whatchacallit? The patriarch. Dammit, my children are gonna come to me!"

And I believe him: at last the lowering of the promised boom.

On the ride back home to western Pennsylvania, Mort and I and the kids have fun with this. "A patriarch!" Mort shakes his head. "So Joe wants to be a patriarch." In a forced baritone, my son says: "Let the decree go out. All issue must return to the ancestral castle." It's a sparkling morning in late May. That and the silliness make us feel glad and slow us down. We arrive half an hour late.

Everybody is out on my parents' lawn except for my father, who, we are told, is inside calling the state police and the hospitals. I bear-hug my baby brother's expatriated bones. He shoves his two little girls into my embrace: *Look, Shang, see what I did!*

My mother, who for her fiftieth birthday asked only that "from now on" we call her Lois, looks nervous and dizzy. All these people loose in her garden, making free with her house. Once we had all left home, that twenty-five-year rupture in her life sealed, she opened the door to us with only the thinnest attempt to conceal her . . . the only word is *terror*. As though we were tax collectors or thieves and she utterly without succor.

Down the back steps comes my father, his cigarette dangling from a black plastic filter. The gruesome visions are still fading from his eyes but he would never admit he'd had them scooping our parts into heavy-duty Hefty bags. He doesn't even say hello. He says, "Your Aunt Peg asked us all out to the farm this afternoon."

The smallish suburban bi-level behind him is not the house in which we grew up, so if there is an Old Homestead, I suppose it must be Peg's farm, which had once belonged to my father's parents. Peg and Eddie Maguire were young there once, in the fifties, when we were kids. They loved company and the O'Baras were happy to oblige, piecemeal and in their multitudinous entirety. Uncle Eddie died at thirty-five and eventually Peg remarried. She and Karl moved to Long Island but kept the farm and, only recently, after years away, came back here to stay. The invitations started going out again, and for the day at least, Lois has lucked out.

We are all milling about on the grass, my father walking in circles. The children, the grandchildren: He is confused with pride. He might have chosen to grieve for us. He's a man who raised three Irish Catholics and, for his trouble, ended up with a Jehovah's Witness, a Unitarian, and a lackadaisical Jew. (One Friday at a foot-long stand, the three of us screeching and wailing until he threw away his hot dog. He needed meat "to keep up his strength," he said. He'd need more than strength in hell, we scolded.)

In a way, we're hardly even Irish anymore. Patsy's a Haddad now and divorced. I'm a freckle-faced Rosenthal. Somewhere along the line Bud dropped the O from

O'Bara, although I'm not so sure anything given is ever discarded.

And besides, how could my father have afforded such an incontestable grief when we were the only self he had? Whatever we were had to be entirely negotiable, could become at any time the norm, the ideal, the desirable everything. What we lacked, he provided; it embarrassed us sometimes how he stretched us for strangers, supplied missing medals, added dollars to salaries, honors to degrees.

He walks stiffly, older than his sixty-two years. He lets everything have a go at his body—colds, arthritis, constipation, "the grip." Because of his fine bones and perennial thinness, he's always seemed taller than he is. Arms and legs sharp as scissors. A long drink of water, my mother used to call him when she wanted to be fond.

"Now pipe up," he says (meaning *pipe down*). "Let me tell you how we're going to do this. I'll lead because I know the way. Patsy, you next—get that oil checked yet?" She nods and grins. He points to my husband: "You can take up the rear." Mort whispers to me, "This could mean forty years in the desert, maybe more."

Everybody starts scrambling around; the families get shuffled. This one wants to ride with that one; the big girls argue over the baby girls. A comforting discord. I yank aside my son, the wrestler: "Lord knows what your Pap told everybody. If someone says you're a state champion, you are. Hear?" My daughter grabs one of Bud's babies and hops into Patsy's Olds. Bud's wife goes with Mort. I get in the back of Dad's Subaru with Bud.

It's a forty-minute ride to Peg's. Living closer to the

coast now, I have nearly forgotten what it is to be met
by mountains, these round, agreeable Alleghenies, this
road cutting a modest lateral scar across the upper slope
of the shoulder that runs down to the Lomahoming Gap.
Perhaps as a child I never knew that in its habit of un-
ruliness and wildlife surprise, this route was also lovely.
Sunlight spears through new leaves. Deep in the gorge,
the river cool with jewels and shadow. Bud has thirsty
Southern California eyes; he fills up on green, green,
green, sips the mossy darkness bottled between the trees.
"Was it always so, so . . . ?" he whispers. "No," I say.
"Of course not. It used to be home." The perfect thing
to say. The perfect afternoon. He hugs me again. Was
there ever a time of less than perfect gladness?

"Did you run the sweeper under that there Frigi-
daire yet?" My father asks. The question is for me. "I
told you how the dust gets down in that motor. . . ."

We smile, even Lois, for whom these picayune atten-
tions have long since turned tedious. Bud throws his
arms around his dad's shoulders. "Same old worry-
wart."

My father's life wobbles from loose banister to sharp
radiator cover to rusted muffler. A domestic inspector,
he follows behind the babies checking diapers, taps the
rafters for termites. Always early. It used to be he was
merely on time. Then, realizing that people, anticipat-
ing his promptness, might inadvertently arrive ahead of
time, he began to show up early; and then, figuring they
would anticipate his earliness, he began to arrive even
earlier.

My brother is thirty-two years old. He calls me often
from California. "I'm afraid he's going to die," he will

blurt, near tears. We both know it's worse since the business with the Bureau.

If a person works for the state, they say a person should not be surprised. When it began—when it became clear my father was being groomed for professional extinction—when with snubs and incivilities and fiendishly subtle pressures they began to nudge him out of his job with the Rehabilitation Bureau, the three of us, his children, came clawing out of our domestic stupors. We wrote to editors and congressmen, made scurrilous phone calls, levied threats, screamed and cursed and carried on. It was good for us. The day my father resigned *we* felt betrayed. "Just so much water over the bridge," he said. We thought he should have loathed the bastards at least as much as he'd loved that job. He put on his early retirement like a magic coat that could make him disappear or, at the very least, cover his shame.

We tried to puff him up with attention. Bud sent him monogrammed shirts from California, named his first daughter Josette. I bought him nothing but silk and cashmere. I assigned him his very own color. "With those sapphire eyes, doesn't he look smashing in blue!" I'd gush. He clung to his namelessness and hung his elegant bones with soiled polyester. Though I must admit, in time, he could be tempted into vanity by a gift of baby-blue.

He fell over my mother's waning years like somebody standing in her light. He slept a lot. He grumbled. Visions of faulty wiring and filthy refrigerator motors hammered him awake in the middle of the night. I knew Bud didn't fear his being hit by a car as we did when, as children, we noticed he didn't look both ways. Or cancer, except, as they say, it can start with the smallest spot of melancholy. Whatever Bud feared couldn't be cautioned against, cauterized, or cured. It was a letting go of vitality like the slow escape of air, as if he could steal his leaving past us as we slept.

The road is dappled and dancing. We delight our parents with the news they mercifully missed years before: the time Bud almost took his motorcycle into the stone quarry. "Here," he says, "here's where me and the guys used to drag." "I used to dive off those rocks," I proudly announce. Caught up in the spirit of reckless confession, my father says, "See that little nook over there. Before we were married, your mother and I used to park there and, you know, uh, smooch."

"Joe!" cried Lois. "What gets into you?" Bud and I crack up and my father is drawing his upper lip down over his teeth, out of habit, the way he used to stop his smile before he got dentures.

Now his eyes keep darting suspiciously to the rearview mirror. Finally he says, "That's it! We're pulling over. Damn Patsy doesn't have sense enough to wad a paper with." The little car bumps onto the berm. My father gets out. The ubiquitous cigarette in its holder makes him look brittle, like a terrible actor trapped in a *Masterpiece Theatre* production. He walks back to Patsy's car. "Can't you keep those girls in their seats?" he scolds. "Want a coupla dead kids to contend with?"

Lois shudders openly. "Honest to Pete, he embarrasses me anymore. Always saying things without thinking. Why, you can't imagine what I go through. Last week we had the Trimbles over and out of the clear blue he said he never minded being skinny because fat people would just rot more."

Rot more has a natural echo, a way of hanging up in the air, then turning unexpectedly, ruthlessly funny. Bud and I start to giggle and snort like seventh-graders. Lois clucks her annoyance, bites her thumbnails. My father climbs back in with a magisterial look, a delicious smugness that makes Bud and me exchange doting glances. *Isn't he something?*

The two cars pulled up behind are full of bright faces and waving hands. My husband shrugs. His grin says *Don't ask me. I'm just schlepping after the patriarch.*

The long stretch through the mountains is past; the land opens. Nudged by the notion of space, arms and legs uncoil, torsos lengthen. The car slows, almost as if my father forgot to keep pressure on the accelerator, the same way he forgets to keep pressure on his words; hunched over the wheel, he appears to be watching something through the upper curve of the windshield. There's some spiky marshland, then a strip of black pines, and high over their ragged tops a row of parti-colored kites on taut lines. "Geez," he says. "Hey!" He shakes his head slowly and begins to pick up speed.

I don't know why but we keep blowing ourselves out on small enthusiasms—Bud and I. The cows on the hillside, the baby goat by the fence, the way the red barn is showing through the white one. "Oh, look at that!" Up and down; I am exhausted from rising to an insupportable passion. And just to give myself a break I say, "Hey, Dad, didn't we used to go out old fifty-six and down through the township?"

My father squints out Lois's window. "I guess maybe

19

we did. Peg said this is the best way now. Twelve, fifteen years, things change. Hell, they're always trying to
mess a person up. Just as you think you know your way
around, they move something—say, isn't this a honey
of a car?"

"A little tootsie," I say.

"Good-riding car," he says.

"We always had the neatest wheels in the neighborhood, Dad." I recognize Bud's voice; it's the same one
Lois used on us when she wanted to "try a little psy-
chology." "That Willys Jeep station wagon. Hey, Shang,
remember the Henry J and the big green . . ."

"Thirty-eight miles per hour on a trip." Nobody
bothers to correct him. We know he means "gallons."
All his faculties are turned down, pilot light on low. It's
too much bother to grope for the right word; not
enough power to generate sense.

"See, kids," he says, "the Christmas tree farm we used
to pass is down there somewhere . . . the other side of
the turkey sheds. Now they cut all that out. . . ."

Bud says, "Zat right?"

We come to an intersection. "Now I'm pretty sure we
make a right here."

"*Pretty* sure?" Lois pipes.

"Hell's bells, woman! I was raised in this county."

The road is newly paved, smooth and sticky as licorice. We ride and ride, the riding a near gustatory
pleasure. Finally, my father decelerates again. "Now
wait," he says vaguely. "I think maybe we should have
made another right back there by the ice-cream cone."

"The ice-cream *stand*, Dad?"

"Yep, now I remember." He flips his signals on in

plenty of time for the others to slow down. We back into a cow path and turn around. Next Patsy. Then Mort. Their cars are full of face balloons. I watch their smiles float by and around to our right. The children cannot believe their luck. We are all delighted to be a little lost in a near-country.

Slowly the cavalcade rolls back down to the ice-cream intersection. In the middle of the turn my father comes to another, uncertain dribble of a stop. "Here comes a car, Dad," Bud offers, too quickly for my money. "Why don't we ask where we are . . . just to be sure."

"Think I'll ask the guy in this car," my father says then, making me think somehow of his fondness for game shows and his guileless cheating—his way of grabbing the answer on the way out of the contestant's mouth and believing it to be his own.

He makes a slipshod gesture—half-wave, half-swat— out the window. The driver keeps going until Lois leans on the horn. He backs up. Our party is blocking the intersection anyhow. My father gets out. As soon as he's out of earshot, Lois turns around. "He does this all the time."

"Look, Lois," Budd says, "I want you to get out of the habit of running him down."

"You don't know what I go through."

"Don't you understand? The man has no self-esteem. It's our job to keep building him up, get him to believe in himself." I don't know where my brother's face found the bones to support a look so prim and patronizing; it's more like Patsy's Jehovah's-Witness-don't-say-shit-in-front-of-the-kids face. I am even tempted to feel sorry for my mother, whose hurt eyes will never cry, but we have always known whom to protect. "Don't start in, Lois," I say softly. "Please."

Behind us my father is directing the others into the left arm of the intersection. "Come on, back up," he's barking, with the laconic, restrained exasperation of a traffic cop. "Give me some room to pull around." As if it's all been a simple matter of their following too close.

"What'd the guy say?" we ask when he gets back in.

"Who? Oh, him. Hell, he doesn't know jackshit." Lois smirks but doesn't say a word. Recently she'd said to me, "Honestly, you wouldn't know your father anymore. The language!"

We are back on the road. The sun is before us, a quarter quadrant past noon. The hours and the day's dust have deepened the light; it licks thick as a tongue at my skin. After a while we turn onto a highway nobody's ever heard of.

"Hell, this can't be right," my father says, irritation creeping into his voice. "Damn Peg doesn't know where the dickens she lives if you ask me."

"I don't know about you guys," my brother says, "but I haven't had so much fun in years." He does a little rousing gesture with the fluttering fingertips of his upturned palms, contorts his face at me. "Oh, right," I pick up on cue. "This is more fun than anything."

"Why don't we look for a place to call Peg," Lois ventures.

"Yeah, I'll tell her to put Ed on this time."

"Karl, Joe—it's Karl! Promise me you won't get *that* wrong."

We stop at the first likely-looking place, a combination tattoo parlor and service station. Both appear closed,

22

but to the side of the building there's a set of wooden steps leading to a second-floor apartment. Patsy and her two girls, each carrying one of Bud's babies, troop up to go to the bathroom. My father stiff-legs after them. I am amazed when somebody opens the door and actually lets them in.

After five or six minutes they start to trickle out again. My father comes last. He walks over to the car, pokes his head in the window. "What's my sister's new last name again?"

"Oh, Joe!" my mother groans, her voice straining at the limits of her right to be peeved. Bud and I are gone—choking, snorting, barking out of control in the back seat. Like a kid with an audience, my father tries not to grin.

"Wardell," she says. "W-a-r-d-e-l-l." The back seat moans for mercy.

He gimps back up the steps. When he comes down again, he's walking more importantly. He slides behind the wheel, twists around, smiling. "Hell, we're practically in their backyard. What'd I say back there? Huh?"

We wait for a flatbed truck to clatter by. Then the cars swing out onto the road, simultaneously, catching the sun like the wings of three planes dipping in formation. I shiver in the shadow of a strange thought: How long have we been rehearsing for this?

Daydreaming or whatever he does wherever he is, my father manages to chug right by his turnoff. Three. Two. One. We all back up, pull around and start down a narrow paved lane.

Back on the right track, moving smoothly now, Lois, Bud, and I chatter easily in the aura of renewed faith.

Just as he passes a turnoff leading through a cluster of white farm buildings, my father slows down. "I don't think that was the road," he mutters.

Lois says, "Well, where did they say you make your next turn?"

"Uh . . ." He cranes out both windows. "I'm looking for . . . hell, you can't tell, everything's so overgrown. . . . Who'd want to live out here in the sticks? Damn depressing, those little pipsqueak porches . . . makes you think of undertakers trying to get the goddam body out. . . ."

"See, I knew it! He never listens. . . ." With shaking hands Lois lights a cigarette, immediately stubs it out.

She's right. He would have listened for the first checkpoint in those directions, then slipped down beneath the voice speaking them. Heard nothing or only as through water or under ice. That's how he never listens. We all know it is true. "It doesn't matter crap, you guys," Bud says. "This is much better than being there." Also somewhat true. And it is true that Bud's voice is wearing raw as a rubbed heel. Sometimes I am shut out by the utter density of truth and people think I am not paying attention.

My father says, "Hell, yeah, anybody could get screwed (screwed up?) back here. New roads. They make them all in circles anymore. You know that darn Peg was a little troublemaker even when she was a kid." (In that flashy family picture she's the babe-in-arms, a favored Brown Eye, banana curls, big stiff bow.) I look at my father's profile, the silvery hair curling at his nape, the sharp Gaelic features; he is his father exactly, without

24

the pride polishing his cheekbones and, of course, without The Gift.

"Darn right!" from Bud as Lois retreats into a chastened, resentful silence.

In front of a lettuce-green bungalow my father pulls over. "Okay," he says, resolutely: from now on he means business. In the middle of the yard there's a chicken house and a tidy truck patch. "I'll ask these folks if anybody knows where the Wardell farm is."

"Say Maguire," my mother says. "It's probably still known as the Maguire farm."

"Mention both," I say, suddenly rich with opinion.

The others pull up behind. The doors to both cars fly open and Patsy's girls jump out and go flapping down through the yard to the chickens. Bud hollers, "Hey!" His voice is a shock to the languid landscape. "Get back here. This isn't the farm! This is *not* the farm!"

My father goes to the front door, the side, the back. Nobody home. He comes back older than when he left. He walks halfway back to where my husband is parked. "Don't worry, Mort, Dee," he calls halfheartedly. "It's around here somewhere." Then he returns to us, stands for several moments alongside the front fender. Visoring his eyes from the sun's glare, he looks up the long gradient that lies before us. The road continues up that way, narrower and unimproved, and halfway up there's a small ranch house sitting not far off the road.

He walks back toward the others. "Wait here," he says. "We'll be right back. I'm going up and ask the guy in the yard."

The three of us hang forward and peer through the

Subaru's windshield. "What guy?" Bud says.

My father gets in and without another word starts up the hill. It is steeper than it looks. Even in second, the engine lugs. We pull onto a gravel driveway. "Now, where the hell did that fella go?" His voice sounds muffled and enervated. He gets out over our objections: "Dad, the house isn't even finished yet. Nobody lives here." A cement mixer sits stolidly in the raw brown yard. He steps over aluminum ladders, buckets, odd lengths of lumber. He goes to the door, presses his face to the windows.

The light is piercingly bright and up here there's a sharp wind. A wiry whine in the distance, and nearer, the rattle of unputtied panes, the slap of loose plastic. My father stands in the yard wrapped in fine weather, encased as though in a dream: the kind of dream in which a relative, long-dead, appears in your garden, walking in his old way, stooping to smell the verbena; you are afraid to keep bumping your dream along, afraid even to greet him, so infused are you with his precariousness, even though you know, even dreaming, he is beyond your good wishes.

There is panic in Bud's voice. "Think of something to say," he begs. "Gawd, here he comes." He grabs my shoulders. "Shang, tell him how good he looks in blue."

My father comes to Bud's window. His voice is gruff and fragile at the same time. "Wait here," he says. He looks toward the upper fields. "The thing to do is find the highest point. Isn't that what they say? I'll walk to the top and see if I can spot the farm from there."

"I'll go with you, Dad," my brother says.

My father waves him back impatiently. "Just simmer

26

yourself," he growls. His footsteps crunch down the gravel driveway. In the front seat Lois holds herself impassive as an old squaw.

The dirt road dwindles to a broad footpath, then a narrow one on either side of which are tall grasses, patches of bright yellow—goldenrod and wild mustard. The sky is blazing blue, but flat and unreal as a glimpse of distant ocean. As he walks, the wind picks up, whips his trouserlegs and we watch him try to beat it back with both arms. From out of the brush come two small mongrel dogs. They jump and nip at his heels. He reels away from them, stumbling now and again off the path. Partially hidden among the weeds, near the crest, a rusty Airstream trailer.

"Remember what he started to say before, about us, uh, *smooching* out on the pike?" Lois has twisted around in her seat to face us.

"Well, it was true," she says, "even if he's got no doggone business broadcasting . . ."

"Lois, there's no need to explain . . ." says Bud.

She holds up the flat of her hand. "Once a trooper stopped, you know. He motioned for us to roll down the window and then asked your father his name." She pauses to get our attention because, tracking Dad's progress, we are only half-listening.

"Know what he did?" she presses. "Instead of saying it, he spelled it. Like a first-grader, all nervous and solemn."

"Darn," Bud says. "Did he do that?"

"He spelled it," she repeats softly. "J-o-s-e-h-p."

"Aitch pee!" My brother's laugh is small, sharp, and hurts like gravel in your shoe. On the back ledge he finds a crushed box of Kleenex. He dabs at my mother's eyes. "That's funny," he says in the croaking, crumpled tones of someone trying to make crying sound like laughing, or laughing like crying. Nothing, I'm beginning to see, not even our truest expressions escape adjustment.

Again, we take to our windows. For a while longer he is still climbing, his blue shirt a silky swatch torn from the sky. I think of how it's always been like this with us, useless measures, the ragged bits of bravery. Reindeer still on the roof in July. As a girl I compared my family with neighbors and knew only that I would not have wanted to account for us. Lately, my reckonings are hurried, run to one word, too easy. "Irish," I say.

Even I. Even as my father struggles against the grade, I am electing the words to frame the moment, my head full of empty white landscapes, the empty white music of my grandfather's Gift. The air is lucid and lonely as wind chimes.

I watch him ease up against that luminous blue. His arm, raised perhaps to shade his eyes, makes a shape like a single, dislocated wing. His body looks slim and young, limber as a sapling. It must be a heat mirage, a trick of distance, but don't we all see him make that scissoring leap over some indeterminate hurdle? A rock? A tuft of yarrow? Then several steps more. A silver trailer. The jagged, uncertain seam between earth and sky.

We do not speak. My brother curves his palms into a white basket and the three of us watch how swiftly the afternoon runs through his fingers. Bud leaves the car and walks to the center of the lane that runs downhill to the waiting cars. Now he cups his hands again, around his mouth, gathers his voice to a bellowing panic that funnels harshly down the valley. His arms start to flap in some kind of disjointed semaphore, private and primitive. "Get up here," he hollers. "Now!"

I follow Lois onto the trampled path. At first the hill's upper shoulder blocks our view and finally we spot my father again, his shirt flapping and ballooning, full of wind and impatience. Behind me the unseemly sound of pockets, keys and coins. I spin around and my brother's eyes squint snippets of O'Bara blue. He looks right through me.

Some fifty yards behind, Patsy hurries after us with long evangelical strides; Mort, still further back, walking briskly as a banker; come Patsy's girls, single file, airplaning in tandem; comes my gentle wrestler bearing Bud's baby on strong shoulders; lagging behind, near the road, my daughter, her hand grabbing back to Bud's three-year-old, who comes last, stumbling, tilting like a tiny drunk. The whole straggling, untidy lot of us, a knotted tail dragging determinedly uphill.

Now with his back to us, my father, Joseph, his color straining against color, a form in flux, billowing, lifting, lifting . . . and I have to double forward against the lurching tug on my breastbone, the dearth of breath.

Fingers splayed across her chest, Lois, my mother, turns to me. "By now, he must have seen the farm," she says, her jaw rocking softly. "By now he's seen."

Best Quality Glass Company, New York

When I reach the Dunkletown exit on I-78, I am not thoroughly astonished to be there. Familiar roads, routine trips, have a way of sopping up time, removing the driver from his tired distances, so that he arrives and has not traveled farther from his mind than its side porch or, if you will, the palm of the Hand holding him to the road. Ordinarily, having left my office but milliseconds before, I arrive at this far point stunned with a sense of sudden, violent dislocation. When did I pass the brewery? What happened to Breene? New Lorraine? Time and space seize on me, cover my tracks.

As I said, this does not happen today. All the way home I have counted off the landmarks, cursed the exits for not showing their tedious faces sooner. More than the western terminus of a daily habit, a conditioned reflex—today, at least, home is a destination.

The difference is I don't know what I'll find when I get there. Either Wilda's car will be there or it won't, and in either event it will come as a great surprise to me. *There!* she'd say, further evidence that I don't know my wife at all. Shouldn't I, after sixteen years, have developed a sense of her? Her style, her patterns, her limitations? Would she leave me for more than a day?

Other times she went off in a cloud of dust and was back before the dust settled, looking contrite and ashamed for leaving. Or maybe for coming back. But lately she's different, lives closer to the windows, stops with her teeth in the apple to listen, walks on tiptoe: *Was that the phone? Is somebody at the door?* An outward leaning, as if she might finally have somewhere to go.

Something else needs to be settled, a second surprise, so to speak, and that's how I'm apt to feel about the first one. I'll come up over my long, freshly paved, licorice-smooth driveway, crest at the paint shed and look down through the pines to the house. Either my heart will leap up or sink to new levels. Or I'll go about my business as usual. And I haven't a clue as to which possibility might engage which response. Last night I wanted to kill her. Who knows about today? Last night I smashed lithographs and mirrors instead of her skull. Today I am mild as this late March drizzle—a harmless fellow, looking for home.

Her dirty white Vega, that worthless piece of junk she refuses to trade in because "it's done nothing wrong," is not in the driveway, nor in the garage, nor in the turnaround behind the rose garden. So intent am I that I fail to notice right away what *is* there: a cruiser car smack dab in front of the house and two people, the state trooper and my son, running around kicking at the cellar windows.

I am not alarmed. Rather I feel quickened in the face of a question more intriguing even than the Wilda problem. Seeing me, the cop comes over to the car. He motions with the flat of his hand. *Stay where you are.* With his fingers he makes circles in the air. *Roll down your window.* I say, "Yo. What's the story?"

"Not to worry, sir, but you've got an intruder in there who won't come out."

"Won't come out?"

"Your boy here discovered him in the basement."

"Justin's always been a little . . . uh, whimsical."

"Not this time. Saw him with my own eyes through the hole in the floor."

"Oh."

"Do yourself a favor." He scratches under the visor of his cap. "Your girl's down at the neighbor's. Kid's just showing me the layout here. Take him down and wait till you hear from me. Got a call in for reinforcements. This guy could be—well, he could be anything."

My boy is reluctant to go with me. He wants to hang around and "do his part."

"We can't be responsible," the cop says, and Justie gets in beside me. He is twelve, thirteen maybe. His limbs just hang there, taking on bones. On the way down to Sprecher's he tells me what happened:

They'd heated up some leftover chili for supper. Hollis made some Pillsbury crescent rolls. (Hollis is smaller but older by two years.) I didn't ask why they hadn't bothered to wait for me. Apparently she went upstairs after supper and then the phone rang. Justin answered it, hoping to hear his mother's voice. It was "a guy from the I.R.S." with a message for me he can't recall just now. Just before hanging up he noticed light coming from the hole in the floor near the staircase around the corner from the basement door. Puzzled, he went over to investigate. To his horror he saw a face staring up at him from the room that was once a coal cellar. "I just wanted to get the heck out of there," he says. But then he remembered Hollis, innocent and unadvised on the third floor. (The kids live in the attic. With the completion of their rooms we ended seven years of renovations to the old place.) He found her on the john, memorizing the map of Africa. Shoeless and shaking, she followed him to the second floor bathroom, out the window, onto the porch roof and down the smooth trunk of the sycamore. Fearing the length and openness of the driveway, they took the shorter but steeper footpath that runs down over the wooded hillside to the township road below. The thawing ground was wet and cold, slippery in spots. Hollis cried, "My toe, my foot!" It rained softly through the bare trees. They had almost reached Sprecher's bungalow when Hollis realized she wore only a pair of blue jeans and a persimmon-colored bra. They called the police from Sprecher's.

Again, I have arrived at a point and missed the passage there. I am stung with strangeness. Even my boy Justie seems to have slipped off his own center and I hardly know him. I try to visualize my house, those downstairs rooms I paint with dedicated regularity, the floor beneath which the intruder bides his time. Is he living down there? Other houses crowd my brain, laying out crisscrossing floor plans. The hole in the floor? Of course! That opening in the black varnished wood through which the water pipes rise to the upper floors. The metal collar won't stay put, keeps riding up, exposing the gap. Of course!

I see better the rooms where we fought last night: the bedroom, bathroom, the guest room, the hall. She secretes her fatal flaw up there, where nobody sees but me: the defiant banners of her carelessness waving from chests and drawers, towel racks and doorknobs, the beds unmade.

She wanted to talk. I, of course, wouldn't let her. I know that once we get down to syllogism, I'm a beaten man. I took a crap and pretended it was a rough one. I hid behind a book, behind a transcendental calm, behind closed eyelids; I can sleep at the drop of a truth-seeking syllable. She said she couldn't bear to see herself reflected in my eyes. I said, "My eyes are closed." She said, "Your eyes behold me darkly. I have no sharp lines, no illumination."

Justin says now, "Did you hear from her today?"

"Did you?"

"No."

Sprecher lets us in, nodding gravely. These are the worst of times. His house is small and the air thick with the accessories of his dotage: liniments, salves, mothballs, cheap wine. On the stove is a dented aluminum saucepan, a glob of cold oatmeal, gray and unthinkable as a massing of cancer cells. My daughter sits with her hands loosely joined on the white enamel tabletop. Her usual dignity has not deserted her, despite the fact that she's wearing Sprecher's long underwear shirt.

"They got him?" Hollis wants to know.

"We told him to come out of there with his hands up and all, but he didn't even answer. Cop called the barracks for more guys."

"Why'd he do that, Just, when he had you helping flush the guy out?"

"Can it," Justin says without real malice.

Sprecher suffers their banter in silence, his hands

tucked under the bib of his overalls. But he's got that squarish, bulldozer look he gets just before his patience runs out. "I never wanted them people in the first place," he finally breaks in.

I am afraid to ask. "And what people might they be?"

Red-rimmed eyes grab at me; his tone beats after my ignorance, whipping his basic Pennsylvania German into a frenzy of high flat quacking like a duck. We finally understand him to be cursing the state school up the road.

Justin's eyes widen. They are depthless blueberry-blue, like Wilda's. "That's gotta be it. Retards! Ya shoulda seen him, Dad, the way he looked up at me." Throwing his head back, he demonstrates an empty, upward stare; mouth a slack wet gaping hole, eyes vacant.

Hollis shivers openly and Sprecher starts to quack again. "I knowed it!"

Sprecher is an angry old man, staying alive on oatmeal and rage and the summer work we throw his way. He mows our lawns, prunes the orchard, helps Wilda in the gardens. Most of the time he's furious with us, too: the kids fooling with his equipment, leaving baseball mitts and lawn games in the path of his garden tractor, the dog stealing his molasses cake, Wilda forgetting to buy grass seed. But mainly his anger takes broader aim. He hates earthen dams and Russians, injustice, the medical profession (because it refused to save Jenny), and the government. When he was still farming, they made him destroy a hundred head of tubercular dairy cows, the same government that today brings us cretins in the basements of honest working country folk.

"Can't keep aholt of them kind. Too gotdem dumb to stay put. . . . Saaaay, where's the missus?" Just because he squints and smiles slyly, does that mean he suspects me of something?

I look to Hollis to see what she's told him, but I should know better; she's close-lipped as I. We are hoarders of secrets. Her face has no key. I decide to take the humorous route: "She's hunting small game with the daughters of Diana." Sprecher likes a joke.

"Oooooo-uh," he laughs. "And ott of season! Oooooo-uh. Yeah, well, tell her there's a bigk squirrel in her cellah."

The first year Sprecher worked for us he stopped by one morning. When Wilda answered his knock, he told her they had just announced over KVNR the start of World War III.

She said, "They already gave it a name?" Then she asked the agitated old farmer in for fruit-ade and together, they waited for the first bombs to fall.

Maybe it's crazy Wilda in the cellar because she had nowhere to go after all. Wilda, maddened with hunger, loneliness, and talklessness, reduced to a twisted nubbin of her former self. Still shell-shocked, maybe, from last night.

She'd wanted things settled one way or another. Would I let her go then, if I could not love her? For the sake of her soul, no less. She knows I can't be led kicking to the well of such alternatives. Am I obligated to be her liberator as well as her looking glass? "My, my," I said, "If you're so perfect, when was the last time you put the toilet-paper roll on the holder? Why is there a jar of basil on the highboy?" This time she wasn't so dumb as to answer these questions. She pressed on. I kept saying "Listen to yourself!" and she started getting tongue-tied and talked anyhow, tied of tongue. I gave her the customary warning shot: a couple of snapped pencils, a magazine whipped to the floor. Nothing seemed to sink in. She just stood there oozing pop-culture verbiage like a toothpaste tube jabbed full of holes: honest emotion, psychic pain. "I'm suffering," she said. "*I'm* suffering," I said and closed the subject. One by one I took her Curriers from the bedroom wall: "Mother's Pet," "Little Ella," "Birth of Our Savior," "James K. Polk." Against the walnut newel-post at the top of the stairs I dashed them to smithereens. Shattering glass comforts and composes me, scatters my afflictions. But I needed more: a spotty water glass, the jar of basil, then the old gesso mirror from above the dresser in the guest room. Down the hall Wilda stood with her head in her arms. The kids were up, defending her, too. I took the mirror to her like an offering, held it up to her barricaded face. "Behold!" I said and read the yellowed paper label peeling off the back: "Best Quality Glass Company, New York." Then I marched triumphantly down to the newel-post. Silvered shards didn't fly but clinked heavily around my feet, down the first few steps. It wasn't at all the dramatic spectacle I had in mind.

"Oy—look it!" says Sprecher from the window. We all go over and watch two more patrol cars glide by like flickering ships through the mist of the early darkness. We follow the path of their lights, blurred red disembodied balls, plucking from oblivion the entrance to our grounds, the lane's upward turnings.

"Poor dumb guy!" Leave it to Justie to pity the intruder. So like his mother, who feels sorry for cars. Dreamy, absentminded pair. Boy with her face, malleable, unsettled features. No-color blonds; eyes against the pallor are dark stains. Given the nature of things, that each fathering requires an act of blind faith, and even having made that act—when I really think about him, spawned by my seed but untouched by my genes, I can stop loving him for the space of that considered injustice. He, another her! But his awkward stride, the down on his neck. I know no other son and am condemned to drown a little daily in the largeness of unspoken love.

Your children are your children, but a wife is just a smoke. They come and they go, wives. Dry-eyed, they fill plastic buckets with splinters of glass on the way to the heart, bright fragments flashing a trillion angles of domestic aftermath. So the children don't cut their feet, they clean first, run the Electrolux and then pad off into a soft spring night that doesn't sweep them right back in. Nights are not tides.

"How are your feet?" I ask Hollis. She shrugs. Her right toe is cut. Are the woods full of glass, too?

Then they hunker down in your cellar, scaring your kids senseless, settling into the dungeon life while you're still getting used to the patient light of day.

The only light in Sprecher's kitchen is a pink scalloped wall fixture above the table and the illuminated dial of the clock on the stove. The house is chilly. Sprecher must have turned off the heat for the year. In the event of a late March cold snap, he'll layer on the flannels.

"Mebbe one of them smaht aleckys from up they-ah," he says, stabbing a finger toward the blackness outside the window over the sink.

Hollis screws up her face. "Camp Rockbottom?"

"That place for them little city coluheds, chust abott in my back yawd."

"No way! Face I saw wasn't black. Nobody's up there in March anyhow."

"Besides, they're just kids," says Hollis in tones meant to shame and enlighten. "They're not one bit different. . . ."

"Don't tell me no different! They ain't like me. Do I tramp donn an oldt man's sugah peas?" He starts stomping savagely on the cracked linoleum, his finger in Hollis's face. Quack, Quack. "Do I tease his poor oldt dogk, break goot limbs off his poor oldt cherry trees?"

"Mr. Sprecher," Hollis says softly, "why don't you show us some of those pictures you've got of Jenny?"

"Well, I don't know—uh," he sulks, but almost immediately goes back to the bedroom through a faded blue chenille curtain. I shoot Hollis a look to tell her grandchildren about; she lowers her head demurely.

Justin pulls up a chair, his smile sweet and fond for a kid his age. We draw curlicues with our fingernails on the tabletop, stare at the linoleum, cleave to our private images of the stranger.

"What hole?" I say suddenly to Justin. "What light?"

He looks up. "Huh?"

"There's no hole in the floor by the cellar steps." How had his narrative planted my memory with nonexistent particulars, added plumbing, so to speak? There are no pipes coming up through openings cut in the floor, not for a long time. That old dark varnish was covered five years ago with thick plush carpeting, Aztec gold. "And no damn light in the coal cellar either!" I tell him.

"Sure there is, Dad. Tonight there is. Maybe he has a flashlight. He must have drilled a hole, right through the carpet."

I nod, letting him fill my head again with earnestly proposed preposterousness: visions of fiendish little men wielding tiny noiseless implements or, worse, commandeering my Craftsman toolbox while I spend myself in the marketplace each day. Wilda couldn't drill her way out of a cardboard house.

Sprecher comes out with the album, wearing his triumphant little boy look, the one where he tries not to smile. Wilda calls him the old young man, because in his broad cheeks, deckle-edged bangs, his toe-spragging petulance, she sees something of the eternal Katzenjammer kid, give or take several generations of Berks County stoutishness. She keeps coming down here with her bags of fruit and pumpkin breads though it means near-certain entrapment with Our Family Album. Got caught three of four times myself over the years, but I'm better at bowing out, gracefully and otherwise.

He starts as he always does at the very beginning, with snapshots of the first grasses, tender and atremble, at the dawn of creation. Eventually comes Pappy Follweiler caught in the act of coveting his neighbor's barn and attendant hex signs, taking a moment off from the business of begetting mankind and more particularly Jenny, who is soon seen next to her boss at the Rudy Stoudt Shirt Factory and then caressing the fender of a wood-paneled huckster wagon, in the Age of Travel and Technology.

Now, sepia-washed and self-conscious in a lacy Victorian lady's chair, Jenny, the farmer's daughter, waits to become the farmer's wife. "Chenny," Sprecher points, "chust before the weddingk." He gathers himself in the way he does preceding a weighty declaration. "She wass setting right there," he says, nodding toward Justin, "when it happened. Her eyes wass closed, but she sedt, 'Hoyt,' she sedt, 'what will happen to me?' I said, 'Why, I don't know-uh.' " Quick pecking glances from one to the other. If his story has a point, he wants us to get it. His eyes are moist, but whether from rheum or tears it's hard to tell.

Justie walks to the window and comes back. I'm wondering if they use tear gas and if the damn stuff lingers. Jenny, Jenny, you don't ask a guy like Sprecher a rhetorical question with your dying breath.

Leaning across the table, Hollis points to a snapshot. "Who's that, Mr. Sprecher?"

"Oy," he says, "that's Mahlon Herber's youngest." He laughs, blue-gummed and toothless, remembering. "Oy, that young fella wass a pistol." He has difficulty turning the page with his rough, spatulate thumbs. Hollis turns it for him.

When he comes to the farm pictures, I figure it's my turn to check the window. Nothing but the night and the fog. This is the part where he gets mad at us all over again. Jenny and Boots, the German shepherd, in the north field; Sprecher by the giant oak. Sprecher and Jenny planting raspberry bushes. The childless couple in the Primeval Garden.

Out of parodial sequence perhaps, but true to the metaphor lodged in the old man's brain, where all evil began on the day he sold the farm, half to Rockbottom, half to the Fergusons, who sold it to me.

"Them wass goot burries. All ruint now. Canes busted up. Thistles all arount. And my chicken hoss—that hurts me. Swelt up like a det man's belly, bordts sprung-it loose. Next bigk snow, the roof busts in—gootbye chicken hoss!"

I know I should apologize for not taking better care of his raspberry patch and chicken coop, but the sanctity of my home has been violated. I polish the window with my handkerchief and peer out, polish and peer again. Can't he see I am much vexed?

"Barn needs work too. Every gotdem time the wint blows, sheets of tin come shookin' donn off the roof." Let him blow over, I think, hearing the tin come off his rafters. He is all raw, splintery anger, quackety quack.

"Mistuh," he calls, "Who tolt ya to up and rip donn the grape arbor?"

"Wilda did." (Even as I say it, I see her face, begging for the life of those old vines.) "She said the grapes were little and sour. They made lousy jelly."

As I turn toward him, my first thought is he's going to hit someone. His fists are clenched at his sides, but I can't stop. It's like snapping pencils and breaking glass. "It's *my* land," I say.

He looks to the kids, to me, and out toward Rockbottom. His body keeps starting out and coming back. Then he gathers up his album, crookedly, with trembling hands. Photographs pop loose from their corners and flutter to the floor. Hollis and Justin flit around handing them back.

"She chust don't know how to make chelly," he says, sulky but subdued.

While he's shuffling around in the back of the house, Hollis says, "I'm not imposing on his hospitality one second longer," and she pushes us out into the night.

"What hospitality?" I ask. We are three abreast across Sprecher's front stoop. "Did he as much as offer us a glass of water?"

"He gave me his undershirt, Dad," and she starts to cry before thinking better of it. "And what makes you think the land is yours, man?"

Sensing a trap, I answer anyhow, lamely, "I bought it."

"Well, he paid for it," she says, managing to sound triumphant and brave through chattering teeth. I want to put my arm around her but give her my suit coat instead.

Justin is the first to spot their headlights filtering down through the tumbling bank of fog before us.

"They're back," Hollis says tiredly.

"I hope they didn't have to shoot him," says Justin. We run through Sprecher's gate to meet the first patrol car. It's the officer I spoke with earlier, and he's alone. "He's in one of the other cars?" I ask, straining to see through the murk into the vehicles pulled up behind. He shakes his head no.

My God, it *is* Wilda! They wiped the soot from her brow, tweaked her mouth into tremulous little smiles, and left her propped up in bed eating ice cream and watching Baryshnikov on PBS.

He clears his throat and fidgets and reaches into his pocket. "Here's your culprit," he says at last.

I don't understand at first when he holds out his hand, and then, oh, no, I think, oh, no, you don't, if that's supposed to replace the conjurings of the past hours, the whole waxworks of rogues and retards and my wild-eyed Wilda babe. . . .

"I can hardly believe it myself," he's saying and hands me a piece of glass, of mirror to be exact, shaped roughly like the state of Nevada. "Was nestled in the nap of the rug as cozy as you please." Since I am speechless, he feels obligated to go on. "Do yourself a favor, sir. Don't blame the boy. It's a hell of a thing. Had me fooled. Officers Bansky and Heller, too. Didn't figure it out till we went down there after him. *Him?* Ha! Hell of a thing."

When we get home I offer to scramble the kids some eggs. Justie never turns down food. Hollis stands at the dining-area side of the kitchen island, elbows on the rim of the sink. "Not hungry," she says, but makes no move to go up to bed.

There's a silence that needs to be broken; otherwise I can't swallow my eggs, not even with ketchup. I scrape the skillet onto two plates, giving Justie the larger share. "I hope you guys realize," I say, "that if we ever *really* need Pennsylvania's finest, they'll never believe us."

"The kid that cried wolf—is that it, Dad?"

"You got it, son."

"I don't want any eggs," he says. There's a sharp pelleting sensation on the back of my head and a sudden cold trickle down my neck. I spin around and take the shot full in the face. Hollis's lips form a silent curse. She drops the spray nozzle in the sink, where it rests a moment before beginning to crawl slowly back down its hole. Then they both run out of the kitchen.

When the upstairs has gone quiet and the light leaves the branches beneath the kids' windows, I go to see for myself. From my pocket I extract the bit of glass: the state of Nevada, the state of matrimony. The living-room lights are unchanged since early evening. I press it down hard into the untrampled Aztec gold pile here by the baseboard. Immediately there appears a miniature pool of radiance, seemingly lit from below. With more difficulty than I would have thought, I lean cautiously forward until I see what I came to see: the bug-eyed toad; the leering, drooling, demented fool below.

Quickly I draw back out of his view, subterranean wretch! He has always been before me and I have always been on my way here. How is it I forgot? It'll take a while to get my bearings. Believing itself soundless, the night sneaks past my eardrums, but I keep hearing her car—or is it Wilda chanting antiphons to herself as seen in a lover's eye?

She doesn't know the half of it. Sprecher claims my land; the I.R.S. is calling; my children turn on me like hounds; the devil in the basement refuses to come out.

I make myself a drink, sit by the window, and wait for my wife to come home.

The Appaloosa House

My father's girl friend's name was Dolores and my mother went by Dusie because she was one. As in pip, as in pistol, as in humdinger. In those days men waited until after the holidays, so he left us on the second of January while the yabba-dabba-doo cartoons on TV tried, by their jangle of Saturday-morning sameness, to deny it, and just as it was starting to snow.

For three days and three nights Dusie observed an oddly formal time of mourning, in the manner of an Irish wake. She called in her friends; she wept and laughed. There was cake and wine, coffee in the fine Belleek cups that had come from Kilkenny. On the fourth morning she came downstairs and said, "Maybe if I'd kept the trash baskets emptied and got somebody out to paint the house last summer like your daddy asked . . ."

I stopped stirring my Sugar Crisp into whirlpools and rolled my eyes up at her.

"But, oh, no, I have to be Madam Nobody-tells-me-what-to-do, Mrs. Stand-on-my-rights, stubborn Irish smartypants. Maybe if I'd got rid of all the empty olive jars in the fridge?"

We exchanged rueful looks that answered all her silly questions. We alternated weak, well-meaning chuckles and then she put the coffee on. "Did you know he took

46

both bottles of Lavoris?" she said, like it was something she'd read in Ripley's. It was shortly after that that she kicked off the campaign.

Right after breakfast, in fact, she drove us down to Cherry Street; she parked in the loading zone in front of House of deLuca, which was the cruddy yellow brick building where my dad manufactured his line of budget neckties. I waited in the car while she tramped out her message in the strip of snow between the building and the sidewalk. She was wearing a big orange fur coat nearly the same color as her hair. I watched her face turn splotchy as a washerwoman's hands in the cold air. She was that other kind of Irish, not dusky-haired and delicate but ruddy, rawboned, and sturdy as a pack mule. In funny little schoolgirl shuffle steps, her stadium boots tramped along in the snow. The letters were twenty feet high. "S," then "O." She came around the bottom belly of the "B" with high marching steps and finished with a flurry of furious double-barreled stomps. S. O. B.

"Ma-ah!" I squeaked when she got back in the car.

"What?" she said. "What's wrong with sob? You know, sob, sob, sob. Boohoo, the rooster flew the coop."

Next day she called Western Union and made arrangements to have a singing telegram delivered to Dad at work. "What can you give me in, well, a crumb-bum medley?" she asked in the crisp tones of a suburban matron. As carefully as if she were choosing music for a wedding, she made her selections: "Your Cheatin' Heart," "How Come You Do Me Like You Do?" and "Toot-Toot Tootsie, Good-bye."

She called the printer and had him make up announcements. When they came, I helped her stamp and address them. Very plain, very tasteful, which was a distinct departure in a family partial to purple velvet and plaster lawn statuary. But Dusie had the unerring Irish instinct for effect. The message, too, was simple and painfully to the point: MR. AND MRS. NUNZIO DELUCA RESPECTFULLY SUBMIT THAT NUNZIE IS FAT, FORTY AND FOOLING AROUND. NO GIFTS. SEND MONEY. HE'LL NEED IT.

Once we'd get these projects cooking, it was just a matter of time till they boiled over. We lived to hear the affection lurking in the hells and damns of his false indignation. Dusie would take the call on one phone; I'd hang on the hall extension. Or sometimes he'd come by; it didn't take long after the announcements went out. I remember how he went right to the kitchen and, as we stood by gaping, proceeded to make himself a peanut butter banana. It was hard not to draw a mental circle around that scene, hard not to start feeling cozy. A trick, I decided, and for the first time I saw him not as a father but as a man—*somebody's* man—a man with a middle like a flour bag and stumpy legs. His over-large face and well-tended moustache, combined with two great symmetrical wings of thick salt-and-pepper hair, gave him the look of expecting to turn handsome at any moment. Unruly eyebrows and wet brown eyes; he was growing more like a Nunzie every day. I couldn't picture him with this Dolores person, who probably ate corn off the cob in rows and carried Pretty Feet around in her purse. I wished him a speedy old age so Dolores would see that the old rattletrap wasn't good enough for anyone but us.

"Listen, Kathleen (he never called her Dusie when she

was acting like one), I'm just the poor son of an Italian immigrant. How 'bout giving the old boy a break?" Talking with his mouth full meant he couldn't have been too mad. He was a sucker for her stunts and Dusie knew it. She'd always been able to butter him up with monkeyshines, romping through the neighborhood in sheets, baying at the moon like an escapee from the state hospital down the road. And dying. She "died" all the time. Strokes before breakfast, poisonings at lunch; I grew up thinking everybody's mother "did" heart attacks but probably not as well as mine. And Dad boasted the way some men crowed about their wives' cooking. "You're not gonna believe it, Herb," he'd say, rushing the start of another Dusie story.

Several weeks later, after the weather had made that indisputable turn into spring, we went down to Cherry Street and picketed my dad's plant. Dusie had hand-printed a huge sign that read NUNZIE DELUCA UNFAIR TO WIFE AND KIDS. For most of that sweet spring afternoon we paraded up and down the walk, Albert on one side of her, I on the other. She carried ten-month-old Teena Jo papoose-style on her back. The soles of Albert's shoes flapped and slapped as he walked. I was eleven and wearing one of her size-fourteen housedresses cinched at the waist with gold and green Christmas ribbon. Stretched-out bobby sox bunched miserably around my ankles. As an afterthought, she'd tucked the Dr. Denton-ed baby in an onion bag. The worst of it was, Albert and Teena Jo weren't even ours.

"Wait till Mrs. Stefka finds out," I taunted. Dusie was supposed to be keeping an eye on them while their mother went shopping. "You're gonna get it, you're gonna get it," I singsonged softly as we pounded the pavement. I was getting too old to be her loyal sidekick anyhow; I was learning to feel "dumb," especially when a fussing old woman came up and gave Albert and me each an orange and a nickel.

Inside the building, Dad's employees, most of whom knew us very well, kept rapping on the dusty panes. They waved and looked vivified; in due course my dad came out and flagged down the Mister Softee truck. He bought us all frozen yo-yo sticks. Then he whacked my mother once on the behind and went back in.

She packed the next four months with sometimes inspired, sometimes second-rate shenanigans. Nuisance calls to his office in assorted foreign accents. The BEWARE OF THE STUD sign on the factory lawn. She bought us both Orphan Annie wigs that made us look like a pair of dried chestnut burrs. In those and dark glasses we followed Dad and Dolores all the way down to Pimlico in Maryland. They never noticed we were behind them or if they did, didn't let on. Not knowing what to do with ourselves once we got to the track, we ended up going to see *Invasion of the Animal People* at some local movie house. "Lotta good that did us," I said to my mirror image in the theater washroom. Framed in that bonnet of curls, my face lost some of its stronger points. I wanted to think *flowerlike;* I wanted to think *fragile.* I had his dark popping eyes and sloped forehead, Dusie's sharp nose. I remember thinking my father left us for all the pretty little girls in Dolores's belly; he would buy them horses like the one he'd promised me. I dreamed I drowned their children by the dozens, as fast as they were born, but sometimes they were my own babies, and, ashamed, I hid them in sandy coves and giant potted plants the likes of which have never been seen in our city.

When it was, exactly, I'm not sure, but there came a point when Dusie's intrigues broke away from the mainland and assumed a shape, a life of their own. Became, in a way, an island of compulsiveness. She plotted on paper, drew diagrams, made greasy jottings while stuffing pork chops or frying the garlic peppers Dad had shown her how to make. She started jobs and never finished them. She called the house painters and then couldn't settle on a color. So the men went away disgusted. All night long the house creaked with her meanderings, the hall light flashing on and off, and in the morning her eyes would be bright as fever, her body pulling in six directions, her hands too shaky and eager to pour coffee. "Now listen," she'd say (and sometimes I'd only pretend to), "this oughta give the old guinea pause."

In late summer, around the time the three of us would normally be taking a place at the shore, we went down to House of deLuca with two men and a U-Haul. Lucky for us, my dad wasn't around. In the space of an hour we had a cutting table and three sewing machines and whatever else she needed to start a business in the basement, a mini-necktie factory in competition with Dad's. One night I awoke to a gentle pressure on my shoulder and two incandescent eyes beaming into mine. "House of Spouse," the voice said, and the night sifted shut again. My dad claimed such apparitions all the time; they told him where to put his money at the track. But in the morning Dusie was at the breakfast table ordering labels. "House of Spouse," she reiterated. Wasn't it scrumptious? We'd blow House of deLuca right out of the water.

Before Dad booted her out of the office, she used to keep the company books. Not well, I understood, but adventurously. He used to say she gave him bottom lines that would knock Jefferson off Mount Rushmore. I suspect she learned the business better than she let on, because hers was off the ground in weeks. She knew just where to call for supplies, hired machine operators, a cutter; she and I tacked on labels, pressed and packed boxes. Profit being the least of her worries, she was able to call Dad's jobbers and offer House of Spouse 20 percent cheaper than *House of deDummy*, as was her wont to call it. Shameless, she even promoted the idea of a "label with a story behind it."

That brought him around of course. He came up the driveway in his new canary-yellow T-bird. He was wearing a turtleneck shirt, Levi cutoffs, and a wide belt with a chunky gold buckle in some kind of zigzag design.

I kept right on playing "Oliver Twist Can't Do This" against the side of the house and was dying for him to say the ball was leaving marks on the paint so I could crack how his opinion didn't mean beans around here anymore. But he just stood quietly by watching, so I finally said, "A longer line at the waist would make you look taller, you know." I said this in a monotone, without missing a single catch, as if there were no meanness at all behind it.

He noticeably sucked in his stomach. Then Dusie came out and as she strode toward us, he said, "One of these days, sister, you're gonna go too far." Last year he would have boomed this in what she called his hotshot-Italian-husband voice. It occurred to me at that moment that "Italian husband" could be a kind of unstable species, one that outside its element reverted quickly to an original state—soft, sweet, and perfectly defenseless.

"I had that equipment coming to me," she said. "The business is half mine."

"That's true, Duze," he said agreeably. "Mind if I get myself a Coke?"

"Be my guest." Her arm swept a grand gesture toward the house.

"Maybe we can discuss this over a Coke."

"Maybe the sky will rain rhubarb."

"Ah, hell, Duze, always gotta be a wiseacre." He threw up his arms and as he turned to go, I saw that his belt buckle was really three big fat letters spelling YES.

Dad needn't have worried his head about the business. Though we were getting orders and holding our own financially, Dusie soon let things slide out of sheer indifference. There were no major goals in her life, only ways and means to short-term spectacles. She rarely even talked anymore of Dad coming back, but the scheming and stewing went on, a ceaseless scudding across her storm-green eyes. There were days I stood in oblique, reluctant awe of her wreckless creativity and could see that all those external events—my dad and Dolores and heaven knows what else might strike her—were often only springboards to her intractable genius.

I owned an antique toy, a rusty tin man my grandmother brought from Ireland when she was ten. He clutched an enormous curved pole in both hands and rocked back and forth on one toe from a high perch the size of a dime. I never learned to stop doubting the rickety principles that brought him back each time from his heart-stopping dip over the edge; neither did I trust whatever it was that kept my mother sane and both of us out of prison. Especially after the business with United flight No. 101. Up until then, whatever she did at least evinced a token respect for limits, a sense of comic proportion, as though she'd struck some sort of grudging bargain with the conventional world. What happened was this: Somebody let it slip that Dad was planning to take Dolores to Cincinnati on the eighth of November for the Eastern Haberdashers' Convention. So Dusie did what any self-respecting spurned American housewife would do: She called United and booked that Cincy flight solid. And I helped. We spent days on the phone. In several different dialects and in the names of every prominent citizen we could think of—Dr. Ferguson, J. T. Bigatel from the bank—we made reservations. At some point, the girl said, "Goodness, such interest in this flight. Is there something big going on in Cincinnati?"

"Oh, my, yes," I explained. "It's the annual running of the pipkins. We never miss it." I heard my voice and it was unmistakably Dusie's: her puckish expression on my face, her face on my neck, her neck patching red on my body. Her body standing smart as a new broom in my shoes. My shoes. A pair of dirty white sneakers and a broken shoelace. They were mine and they were still on the ground. "Hey, Ma," I said, finally, "isn't the airlines going to freak-out over this?"

She looked at me, recognition spreading like a rash.

She curdled her mouth and hunched her shoulders up around her head. "Oh, Mother Machree," she said between her teeth.

United *was* furious and if Dad hadn't convinced them she "wasn't all there," Dusie would have been in a pack of trouble. What's more, as it turned out, Dad and Dolores had reservations weeks in advance and, as the result of our finaglings, had the whole plane to themselves all the way to Ohio. Not exactly what Dusie had in mind.

It was nearly winter again when my father came home. Maybe in those days men could be driven back by the first rush of cold through the alleys, the beseeching bells of street-corner Santas. He came in and set his two-suiter down on the rug, flopped into his old Naugahyde chair. You'd have thought he'd just come home from work. He seemed limp and shapeless. His skin could have been an ill-fitting suit and inside nothing but sawdust and old rags. And something else—in some imprecise way he looked strangely subtracted, bare.

"Just like that, Bart?" Dusie said, and whatever else she wanted to say wouldn't come unstuck, so she said, "Just like that, Marvin?"

He gave her his cow-eyed look and laid his hands on his thighs, and then I noticed it was his moustache that was so oddly gone and how shamelessly he sat there stunning us with the sudden pale-pink of his unprotected mouth, his naked face.

"Well!" she said, rancor and resolve bobbing wildly around in her throat. I watched her swallow and swallow again. With all her stubbornness and punch, she could be sliced like scrapple.

"What can I say, Duze? You're the best and the craziest. You're the screwy broad I married. I missed ya, kid."

And I would be tough and dry enough for the two of us. "Where's your YES belt?" I said with a dispassion that was not in my genes. "Swinger!"

After dinner he went into his den and sat alone in the stiff December darkness. I came in pretending it was just to bedevil the daylights out of him. I spoke very quietly, my voice gritty with malice, the sugary kind I was good at. "What's wrong?" I said, "Did good old whatsername . . ." and I slit my finger across my throat, "skiiiiick!" His dark sad eyes working against mine made me sick and sorry at the same time. He held out his arms and I went to him, sat on his lap, laid my head cautiously on his chest. His smell: It was like no other and I remembered how the day he left I'd buried my face in his old Woolrich shirt and breathed and breathed and breathed. He began to stroke my hair, his hands falling clumsy as bear paws, hands heavy with the contemptible syrup of his melancholy, and though it is also possible that I only dreamed it, I have always believed the next thing I did was bite him, my teeth digging down into his shoulder until I could taste the fat salt root of all the tears I never shed.

Then I went in to say goodnight to Dusie. She sat on her bed stunned and sunless as a widow. Over the past months she'd lost a lot of weight; her face was round-eyed, a crumple of planes and angles. "He's home!" I said. "He's home," acting joyful, acting like a child. And after a while, in a voice full of the old music—my grandmother's voice, the voice Dusie used only for ominous or solemn high occasions—she said, "The harvest is past, the summer is ended and we are not saved." In the arc of lamplight her hair sparked gold and copper around her lost white face. Katy Keenan, whose mother had come from Kilkenny, and she hung her head and said no more.

And not that night or the next, but soon thereafter, I sat up in my bed knowing exactly what she'd meant by those words: first the loss, then the time of "taking measures"; our mischief had outrun the demons; we were home free and now he was back and now we were at risk again. I was grateful and yet grief made me thin as paper.

Dusie observed a period of mourning much longer than the first. She spoke little and took long solitary walks in the cold evening air. Once I awoke and looked out to see the freshly blanketed lawn already littered with snow angels, each one just her size. She devoured mystery stories and the poetry of Yeats. Calmly, methodically, she performed any chore my father asked. His bereavement, too, went on, over and over again announcing itself in his dragging step, his slow, forgetful speech. It was a sorrow I prayed the Lord to forgive, for I could never.

But then on the morning of Saint Patrick's Day my mother got up and made us all green waffles, and later that week she did something with freshly baked brownies rolled between her palms that made my dad think Miss Kitt, our cat, had used his pillow as a litter box. We were like a house settling, aching down to itself. The creaks of cautious laughter, the night whispers, the easing of protocols; all the old angers and tyrannies cracking back, snapping into place.

Under the penitential circumstances, it was inevitable that I would get my horse. A magnificent Appaloosa we named Dandy Orbit, after the space program I suppose. Dusie and I both learned to ride and though I was at "that age," I soon became another age, the one that preferred to hang out after school smoking cigarettes by the ice machine at the superette or doing the circuit with high-school motorheads. So Dandy-O became my mother's horse by default and by destiny: Was there any doubt that they belonged together? Dusie with her healthy limbs and flaming hair; she sat resolute and proud as a Keltic queen. And later she would groom him and croon softly, gently stroking his mane. Our vegetable crisper was always full of carrots and apples.

And when she wasn't on Dandy-O she was riding the crest of a new wave of eccentricity. She "died" more frequently than ever, staging dreadful falls and electrocutions. I learned never to take my excuse forms back to school without reading them first. On the blank designated "reason for absence or tardiness" she'd write *bubonic plague* or *hoof-and-mouth disease. Saint Vitus's dance.* I looked *triskaidekaphobia* up in the dictionary: *fear of the number thirteen.* I handed it back to her: "Just say I had a cold if ya don't mind." She liked to enter buildings through windows and doors that said DO NOT ENTER but I would not say she was a classic madcap. She did not, for instance, dance naked in hotel fountains or go barefoot to the opera or hire skywriters except that once, to say her name.

By mid-August of that year the house had still not been painted, so Dad said he was going to be in Dallas for two weeks and she'd better have it done by the time he got back. Or else! (The "Italian husband" was starting to shine through.) I remember that as she gave the painters their instructions they argued a little. In the end they shrugged and carried out her orders to the letter.

The evening Dad's plane came in I sat waiting in the yard on the big white rock that said THE DELUCAS in capital letters. Then NUNZIE, KATIE, CONNIE, and MISS KITT in small. I wasn't going to miss this moment for anything. Way down the road already he must have seen because the car started to drift onto the Madsons' grass. Then he continued on up and made the turn into our driveway and the car crept slowly along a short distance before coming to a faltering halt. He got out and stood alongside the car for a long time, just staring. The first section, which included the garage and family room, had been done conservatively enough in a nice polite beige. The rest was painted paper-bag tan and mottled with great splotches of brown and black. His face was dumbfounded; then perplexed. Then he bumped his forehead in the Calabrese way. "An Appaloosa house," his lips said without sound.

I think we both caught sight of her at the same time. On the lower, the garage roof, straddling the peak. Dusie in her western boots and flannel shirt; Dusie with her riding crop. Dusie astride her house in the deep summer evening; behind her the row of poplars like dark feathers against the green and gold sunset.

My father sat down on the rock beside me. He said

nothing, nothing, and then he put his head in his hands and began to cry. "What the heck," I said, tipping my head for a second against his shoulder, meaning to give comfort, "Eloise Bumbaugh's mother still wets the bed." I patted his arm. He wiped his eyes and went in, and minutes later I saw him emerge headfirst from the guest-room window. On his hands and knees he scraped across the sugary shingles. When he reached Dusie he grabbed her belt and untangled his limbs. He sidled in tight behind her, as if he were setting himself snug in the back of a double saddle. He held on, hugging her close, both of them digging in, clinging to beat the band.

It was the summer of my thirteenth year. My parents will not give each other up; they rage and they cling and six years later my father will die in a late-night accident in the company of a girl named Emma Jean Candy. It was a sad house they rode in the dense August twilight, but it was somehow exultant, inexcusably blessed with the grace of their special madness. These things I began to know as I sat forgotten on that flagrant family rock, and still I knew nothing and dared not move or speak for the mysterious forces suspending the thin moon over the black poplars and all the strange and delicate rhythms holding us all safe in this dusky dream, keeping holy the sacrament of balance.

The Dealers' Yard

According to Otto it was a serious mistake to buy the
groceries first. But Otto, Alice remembered happily, was
not along today to point that out. She dropped her last
purchase—a pint of apple butter from the Amish
woman—into her bag and continued back through the
dusky cinder-block building. Past the egg lady. The to-
bacconist, always pacing ragefully in his stall. Past the
fish vendor and the heaps of slithery chicken parts. Because of the fine weather, the back door was standing
wide open. She paused in the doorway, then stepped
out—a long Mother-may-I step—into the Dealers' Yard.

Of course, now she had to lug her bulky sack along
through the crowd. Celery leaves brushed the tip of her
nose as she walked. It was mid-May, a polished glass
apple of a day, the vendors' stands throwing silver, gold,
and crystal sparks, the festive air only mildly rebuked
by the pungence of celery. Though Alice did not, as Otto
sometimes suggested, "diligently choreograph her own
incompetence," she was not above profiting by the ac-
cidental wisdom of wrongheadedness. Now, having done
her shopping, she would not have to extrude her bright
afternoon through the tunnelly dimness of the Farmer's Market, not have to swim for light, holding her
breath as she made her hasty purchases.

It was rare that she bought anything in the Yard. Most

of the glint and gleam came from cheap *new* glass, chrome and nickel. Empty Mateus bottles, cloth monkeys with missing eyes, a bewildering array of oddments. The good stuff she could hardly hope to afford. But she touched everything, even when small scribbled signs implored PLEASE DON'T HANDLE. Her fingers flew out and alit like willful little siskins. They pinged Sandwich glass cup plates, tested the heft of Waterford, stroked old silks and wools, strummed hobnails. She couldn't help herself, she explained, and as a rule the dealers sighed resignedly and let her go. Today a couple from New York watched her handle to excess a fine little Shaker washstand; they smiled and exchanged doting glances, like proud grandparents. "Just keep your vegetable crisper clean," the man told her in kindly tones, "and the rest will take care of itself." Once people spoke, it was hard to move on. Should she invite them to stop by? Promise to write? She would miss them, she said.

At the next space a frizzled old woman presided over a table spread with nests, some empty, some full of plain or speckled eggs. There were pouch types and mud types, even the smart saliva shelf of the East Indian swiftlet. In addition there were teacups and tiny sweetgrass baskets knitted over with delicate threads that turned to silvery puffs in the sunlight; on some examples an oblivious spider was still working. The old woman had turtle shells and several superb hornets' nests attached to broken pine branches.

"Oh, my!" said Alice. "Do you do much business?"

"The nest-and-web-lady always gets by," the woman said evenly. Alice nodded and hurried away.

It was then she spied the pencil sharpener. Never before had she coveted a pencil sharpener. A knot of enchanted people watched the old man demonstrate with a brand new yellow Eberhard. The device was long like a lathe; he turned a wooden knob that turned a metal wheel that set a whole series of other wheels and gears, shanks and shafts into extravagant, extraneous motion. Preposterously complicated and in perfect condition, it was painted black, the original gold japanning still bright; on the base was a name printed in Gothic letters: TITAN POINTER, PAT. 1885. Alice could almost hear the inventor exclaim, "Let's make a day of it! Let's make our points with wit and gladness."

When the onlookers had wandered off she timidly asked the price. The old man had a round open face, impish blue eyes. He wore a shirt of some coarse gray cloth and black suspenders. He said, "Don't care if I never sell this little rascal. Can't take less than ten for it."

Alice blinked and then quickly surveyed his table. Nothing but a passel of grimy oilcans and rusty license plates, some spare engine parts, empty horse-liniment bottles. How had this junk man come by such a prize? She wrote out a hasty check which he readily accepted, cheerfully waving aside her driver's license. Looking around, she waited for him to wrap her purchase. Directly behind him was a small unpainted wagon hitched to a solid gray horse. Perhaps the old man was Mennonite or eccentric. Then she realized he'd been holding the gadget out to her, his face pink with pleasure. She didn't need another bag anyhow. His parting words to her were: "Make all your points with wit and gladness," and as she walked away she felt his laughter at her back, soft as the nudge of a larch branch.

When she got home and showed Otto, he said, "A repro, obviously. The price should have tipped you off. Neither realistically high nor naïvely cheap—the old straddle-the-sucker game." He reached into her grocery bag.

"But it's a pencil sharpener," she protested miserably. "Who would bother to fake . . . ?"

"Cripes!" he said. "Limp celery! The butter's soft!" His eyes on her were dark and injured. "You did the shopping *first*, didn't you?"

If Otto ever tinkered with the sharpener (and Alice knew he was dying to) it was not in her presence. This was a degree of intimacy he would never concede. He undressed in the bathroom and assiduously avoided the demands imposed by his wife's enthusiasms, her treasures. He tied off her delight before it could reach him, join them in something more critical than marriage; by such refusals he kept his margins tidy, remarkably free of her effects. But sometimes at night as he slept Alice would sneak the tip of her index finger against his rib or elbow and, thus attached, feel much less likely to float off the bed, out the window; it was a nightly struggle against the pull of the space between the stars.

She herself found many pencils to sharpen in the course of an average day. The instant she gripped the wooden knob she felt herself click into place. The knob was worn smooth as a tiger's eye; her fingers pressed the countless fingerprints ground into the grain and then she would begin to crank contentedly along, as if she'd tapped into some hidden rhythm, that smooth and

continuous current rushing her quietly past the pull of
long-dead, perversely shining stars.

Who turned the little wheel for the first time? A man,
no doubt; the subject, after all, was pencils. She could
close her eyes and see him, a slim man, a quiet sort. A
lamplighter about to compute on butcher paper perhaps the cost of coal oil. The device was too frivolous
for the earnest young man but she wanted him to have
it anyhow. His life washed over her; his eyes held the
wistfulness, the chagrin imposed on old photographs by
the perspective of time, as if the subject knew, even
then—even as he plumped and preened—knew and was
sorry.

Her own life went on stumbling along in the enact-
ment of reverse procedures. What demon prompted her
to buy the ice cream first, fill the prescription last? She
painted walls from the bottom up, squeezed toothpaste
from the top down. Who told her to put her hiking boots
on before the pencil-straight slacks? "Who told you?"
Otto would cry. "Think you can harass the bejeesus out
of the natural order? Ha! It would take eons of idiot
Alices working full time . . ."

Once she'd tried to get a quart of tomatoes out of the
cupboard without moving the row of bottles up front.
She was stunned and offended when a liter of herbed
vinegar bucked out of the way and smashed on the
kitchen floor. "What's the big idea?" Otto bellowed from
the next room.

But she kept on pushing, probing, assaulting random spots, as if at some unreinforced point reality might
give way like the breast of an earthen dam. The priest
said it was a matter of faith, but when pressed could

not specify whether she suffered from too much or too little.

Later that year she was trundling through the Dealers' Yard with a medium-size watermelon. When she saw the music box she stopped. Its sprightly mechanism could be viewed through a small glass window: Tiny silver teeth plucked the tunes off the back of a rolling brass cylinder. The music was so vivacious and clean it broke her heart. A paper "programme" festooned with a seraphic orchestra was tacked inside the lid. It listed a waltz, a polka, a mazurka and "Wait Till the Clouds Roll By." When the music stopped she said, "Oh, is it terribly expensive?" The man said, "I don't care if I never sell this little rascal. Well, maybe for fifty dollars."

She looked up. It was the pencil-sharpener man. He was and he wasn't. He didn't seem quite so old this time, though he was far from young. She watched the clouds roll across his blue, blue eyes. On his table, the same dismal assortment he'd been trying to peddle in the spring. She bought the music box. "Have you a card?" she asked.

He smiled. "I'm lucky I have a name. It's Toot—T-double-O-T. Now don't be tempted to overwind, Ma'm." Then she had to make two long trips back to the car, one with the melon and one with the music box.

The next day she called an appraiser and discovered the music box was worth many times what she'd paid for it. "Fine," Otto said when she'd come triumphantly to his den, "but isn't it customary to ask these things *before* you buy?"

It became her habit to enjoy the box in the early evenings. The intricacy of the lacy tunes, the grace notes and arpeggios, the virginal clarity. Even if Otto chose to ignore the elegance, the brave-hearted melancholy of the thing, how could he resist the ingeniousness and careful craftsmanship? He held his ears and closed his eyes, waved the notes out of the surrounding air. *Her* listening was breathless and primitive. Deeper than the subtle resonances, deep, deep in the box, she could hear the lamplighter in the dim kitchen, tapping his pipe, paring an apple, pushing his chair from the table. Between songs she heard him sigh, heard him slip out into the early evening air. He never went far, the porch perhaps to feed the dog, to smell the lilacs. She waited for him to come back so she could sleep, her hands floating out in search of a grip on things.

Her mother came to visit. She was enthralled by the music box. "We never had hairlooms," she said. "Just eats and drinks and kisses. An odd toenail or two." She pinched her daughter's cheek. "When you was born the landlady gave you a little china cup. Real purty. It said 'Alice' in tiny pink flower letters. We wasn't the type to look after things, of course. Lord knows what happened to it."

Alice peered at her mother more closely. "Mother," she said, "were you ever into, uh, animal accessories? Cobwebs, bits of antler, that sort of thing?"

"I don't do nothing but get older and brattier."

It was a rare Saturday indeed that Alice didn't go to the Dealers' Yard. Even when Otto was along they'd go back for a short while, he zipping her along by the elbow. "Hurry up," he'd say. "before the fish man sells

67

out of roe." Then she'd follow him into the market, diffidently waiting at each stall, her arms bowed into a basket for his loaves and fish, the people staring at her socks—one black, one flamingo—her heart hiding behind fat purple cabbages. If she tapped the top cantaloupe, would it really roll off the pile? If the butcher plunged his boning knife between her ribs, would she really die? Then Otto would shake her. "Where the Sam Hill is the bag of chicken hearts? You must've left them back at the funnel-cake stand." Then she'd look back amazed they'd not kept pace with her. "Same old Alice," Otto would groan.

Alone, Alice spent hours in the Yard. The greensward went all the way back to the base of the foothills; hedgerows ran up seams on either side: a pocket sewn into the hazy eastern summer. There would always be worlds within worlds and Alice was happily confined in this one. She felt companionable and confirmed, coaxed away from the tyranny of cantaloupes and unholy conjectures. She was among friends (not the dealers exactly; she hardly knew them though she always nodded, peered suspiciously at the nest-and-web lady, who'd added trilobites and talons to her line.) Their wisdom was secret but sufficient; it rose with the heat above their tarnished silver, their crazed queensware; their marble-top stands. Their laughter stuck in cracks and grooves. They hinted that pacts with melons should not be seriously entered into. These the *only* philosophers; the dead were sacristans of Story.

And Mr. Toot. Every week she'd look for him back and across, up and down the rows, but he was never anywhere to be seen. As she walked she might suddenly look up to see his horse nodding sleepily and him, ensconced, arranging his wares. Every week he'd have but one good item and that so fine she marveled nobody else had found it first. She bought the *fin de siècle* fairy lamp, the set of cocobolo-handled knives, the miniature rolltop desk.

Over the years a pattern began to emerge, growing even clearer like the magic ink of a secret code: Each piece appeared to move a step forward in time, another time; each piece, in a sense, crept closer to Alice. The year 1920, for instance, was marked with a 1920 Dr Pepper calendar in mint condition. Each purchase might even have corresponded with an event then or now or begun with a letter of mystical significance or, taken together, spelled out a prophecy or truth, though she never insisted on these implications and Mr. Toot observed an amused silence.

She was easily seduced by the notion of such systems, not the same at all as the body of raw principles that lead to ruined cantaloupe and flaccid celery. In a certain kind of symmetry, riddles hid their soft surprise and stories closed circles with snaps of bright coincidence.

She began to wonder also why she'd ever thought Mr. Toot old. There was about him only an intimation of age; a suggestion, too, of youth. In all respects he was indeterminate as a nun. His voice fluctuated along a scale that ran from baritone to breathy; he used many accents and inflections. She could hold him to nothing but the dauntless good humor she felt free to construe as fondness.

When she had known him for a very long time, he

offered to watch her packages so she could browse as long as she liked. With her potatoes and apples safe on his wagon she would breeze up and down the rows, touching too much, buying too little. She always knew the spurious pieces, made of new material and sold for old; the dealers looked guiltily away from her finger-knowledge. She could detect the heartbeat beneath a real Victorian pendant. The new ones, innocent of history, were cold with earliness.

In their chairs, at their oak tables warm from the sun, on their Boston rockers, their painted benches. A travel as heady as any carnival ride. The days flying, *their* days beating with hers, together, like banners in the wind; their lives soft in her lap or leaning over her shoulder into the eye of an insatiable camera. "I can do better than that," the dealers would call after her when she'd fled, breathless, to the next stand. The dolls, the velvet dresses, the goosewing axes with cracked handles. "So can we all," she'd intone reverentially, in the voice of an acolyte.

It was a party, a celebration. She lifted their goblets; the air would be rich with amberina glints and splinters of cut rubena. Pewter flagons and porringers, not empty but full of emptiness. She tried to explain the difference to a dry little man endlessly arranging his wares so as not to appear to be keeping an eye on her. "Please don't finger the britannia ware," he whined.

Otto was getting older. His hair was gone, his flesh skimpy; it seemed he had dwindled to a spindle of quintessential self about which the world tried creakily to turn. He said, "Don't bring any more junk home."

And he'd argue endlessly, one day on behalf of fat asparagus, the next day skinny.

They'd both reached the stage of life when certain books, certain movies had to be avoided on the grounds they were "upsetting" and time was construed as an occasional gust between the deaths of friends. Between purchases: "Why, wasn't that the same year I bought the old Victrola—six years ago?" "Hell, that was eight years ago, dumbhead, if it was a day. . . ." When of course it had been twelve years by the current calendar.

Through years of practice Alice had achieved a certain virtuosity with her possessions; she worked them like a single musical instrument: turned on what played, lit what burned, operated what performed humble chores, rubbed what merely luxuriated in uselessness. The music she made was always the lamplighter's song: It wove together a hundred melodies; it clung to her skin; it emerged ceaselessly from objects whose physical dimensions turned out to be illusory, for they went on and on, large enough to contain his world, his morning and night sounds, his stridulating grasses and dangerous skies, his solitary rounds at nightfall, his seed exploding in October darkness. He, too, grew old and misjudged the porch steps, the plunge of time. And the ever-evolving song intrigued, absorbed, and softened her. She added details and luminous shadings; into it she blew echoes of Otto, of Otto. Whose song was it? Whose story? Whose face? Edges blurred and she was regularly stirred to a crescendo of longing, a strange, undulating, incalescent love. She'd look around and

71

weep, for there was nobody there but Otto, and she so full, and thus so fragile; she had no choice but to go on loving Otto.

She was wife to one and both. And there were children; she saw them pass like worries across the lamplighter's eyes. And once, late in the day, late in the century, Mr. Toot sold her a lovely porcelain mirror hand-painted in orange and black, depicting a crew team racing under a bright Princeton banner. The men had twenties' haircuts. And when Alice looked in the mirror it rushed like a river, a boat skimming by, light as a swallow. The coxswain looked briefly out at her. His young face with her eyes.

She bought from Mr. Toot a Sears Roebuck catalogue dated 1935. When she opened it, the lamplighter's death slipped out light and dry as the wing of a snake doctor. A flutter in time, a rimple in space. No more. It lay against her lips like a white petal. It slipped into his song like the second voice of a soft country round.

It often happened lately that Otto was not speaking; he'd caught her trying to fork a dill spear horizontally out of the narrow-necked jar. Once too often he'd seen her attempting to walk away before her feet were unequivocally in her shoes. When he spoke, it was to complain that everything anymore tasted like strawberries.

One day in late fall, the kind of day whose warmth is called gracious, when the bony hills embarrass the heart, she was walking through the Yard with a jug of fresh cider. She was thinking how the sun could chill deeper than any wind and when she looked up, there was Mr.

Toot. "I'm thirsty," he said. From her container she filled the cup he held out to her. He drank and handed her the cup. "Here," he said. "It's yours."

"How lovely!" she said, accepting it, turning it in her hands. "Oh!" she said, startled. It said *Alice* in tiny pink blossom letters; *1939.*

She went immediately to the nest-and-web lady. "Look," she said, running her fingers around the rim. "An embroidery frame for your spiders." The woman squinted down. "No, it's just a point in a circle," she said.

"The point where I came in?"

"Perhaps you have a possum knuckle, a hummingbird beak? A lock of hair?"

"Is this where I came in?"

Winter arrived early and Otto was always hungry, though nothing pleased him. If he was going to taste them anyway, he might as well eat them. He demanded strawberries. Alice told him they were out of season but he insisted and she said, all right, she'd go to the market as soon as she got dressed, as soon as she was feeling better. She lay down on the rag rug. *In a second.* "Same old Alice," he sighed. Strawberries swelled and opened like roses, their centers pale as cream.

It must be very early; the Farmer's Market lies hushed and expectant, the air faintly tinged with the scent of strawberries. Lingering from summer? The growing tip of promise? Idling proprietors watch her as she passes; they have the brittle look of people who would secrete strawberries behind stout country hams. In the back of the building many of them are gathered at the egg stand to whisper and sip coffee from a common cup. They do not offer provender of any kind. She draws the wooden door open just a crack and looks out. There is snow in the Yard, snow bristled with old grasses. The hills appear bunched and distant, shoved back like tables pushed away from the dance floor at a wedding. Against the snow the gray breadth of the draft horse is a solid notion. Mr. Toot is sitting quietly at the reins. When she goes back he turns his palms out: *I have nothing this time but hands.* She scrambles up next to him, her limbs supple and willing as when she was twenty.

He takes her home. When she approaches Otto he ignores her. He is peeved with her again no doubt. She's forgotten the strawberries; she's arrived home *before* the car. Same old Alice.

There is a picture window, a frame. The ground is very white and the sky is white; it is all one. Within the frame, a burr of darkness, a photographic deepening, then a clear emergent figure (Mr. Toot?) standing by the curb. He's loading her things into the dray, mindless and methodical as a husband. The pencil sharpener, the music box, the tiny cup. Her hands beat away from her, her fingers probing air, pressing on the white window. In the corner Otto is weeping. The nest-and-web lady croons, "I get older and brattier, older and brattier," croons and collects his tears in a broken egret shell. *Otto, Otto,* Alice calls, her voice splintering into a skyful of sparrows. The window shatters.

Easy the travel and weightless, indelible the taste of snow. Next to her the driver keeps his head lowered as before a blizzard. *Who, whooo, whooo,* calls the wind. *Who?*

Who, she whispers. And waits. *Who?* This is her kind of weather, her kind of question. If she must, she will verge forever on his teasing face, his hidden eyes. What is it if not for the soft shock at the bottom of the story, the gasp of the dimly imagined unfolding wings of finished symmetry? *Who, who,* she says into the wind.

She examines his hands for traces of lampblack. She listens, expecting perhaps the tiny brass beebee tones of "Wait Till the Clouds." "Oh, dear," she says. "You wear your shirt inside out. I never noticed." His larch-soft laugh is like silk on her loins. Her own laugh is bright and new. He speaks but the words gust away from her, for the dray is moving very fast, rushing in ever-widening, ever-softening circles, smooth and silent, far ahead of the prancing horses, saddles of snow on their broad gray backs.

The Horsehair

Mamalou and my father were night fighters. Desecrators, of sorts. I mean the rest of the time they were like water mixed with daylight, elemental next to my skin, benign, colorless. But nights, even as I slept I knew myself to be on call, a red wall pulsing between me and the unattainable absolute of dark.

Conceptually murky—and fearful, perhaps, of finding a name, I thought of these times as *the times. The times*—they were the standard against which I judged the gravity of all affliction. Worse than or not as bad as *the times:* the day I threw up on stage singing "Chiribi-ribim"; Grandpa dying in his painted iron bed; old Doc Beitlebaum, who never heard of novocaine; breaking the class fish tank in my too-short skirt, a big silk poppy at my waist; waiting for polio and Russians. It was an unfair comparison because the ongoing catastrophe always had the edge on awfulness, but it said a lot that nothing bad could happen that didn't immediately invoke the spirit of *the times.*

Often I tried to stay awake until they were safely sleeping. Well past midnight once I was up watching the snow out the window above our bed. Beany's black head on the pillow next to me. Headlights on Logan Street, the angry whine of tires spinning against the unforgiving steepness of our hill (Dr. Deardorff either drunk or coming back from a sick call, or both), his lights fading back toward Manamaugh Pike, the streetlamps in our alley dizzy with fast drumming snowfingers.

The quarrelsounds from the room at the end of the hall reached me first as a kind of scratching, as if the night were a skin on the order of things. I never wanted to separate out the words. I kept stiff vigil at the window: Dr. Deardorff drifting up out of the furry middle distance, on foot, now at the top of the hill, now slipping to his knees, a beggar with a black bag, then up again and on up the alley with high marching steps (summer nights, our window screened, I make Beany play ghost with me, *whoooo, whooo, whooooo,* as he tries to unlock his garage across the alley, *whooo, whooooo, whooo-ooo, I want you, Daddy Deardorff,* in quavering voices, duck down behind the headboard, laughing without sound, half-terrified ourselves).

The voices. *Her* voice mainly, wild as tigers after the slogging silences of her frangible, uncertain art. She had so much wanting; he wanted nothing but the freedom to go on wanting nothing and a little cheddar cheese on his apple pie. With a proud, relentless, luminous rage, she hated his failure to want. It seemed what she wanted most in all the world, next to eternal life and a one-man show, was for him to want . . . something, even a fight, and so she summoned all her strength, her vast creative amplitude, and drove against him mightily: skinny son of a bitch, son of a shanty Irish, cock-o'-the-walk, son of a semiliterate broodmare, no guts, no drive, no wonder he looked pale as death, dead already, slow as dough and didn't he even know, dumb bunny, that Hildie down at the store was robbing him blind, and dumber yet, when the Boyers hadn't paid their grocery bill in months, why was he still letting them have the *imported* provolone and whipping cream . . . ?

She worked extravagantly, with the demonic, febrile urgency of some red-eyed conductor hungry for thunder; led my father unerringly to the crescendo that always came, and suddenly he was unstoppable with wanting. If, in those moments, his gut churned and burned to a sickening shiver of impending pleasure, I know exactly how he felt: He wanted nothing less than to kill her. What he usually did was drill his fist into her face.

Despite our improvisations we could rarely escape that sound. I closed our door that night and tapped feebly on the window at Dr. Deardorff, who was standing in his yard beating at the snow with both fists. The moment her sleeping brain picked up the first signals from their bedroom, Beany assumed her defensive position, drawn up on her elbows and knees, rump in the air, rocking, humming with varying vigor, according to the size of the argument, a tuneless, klaxonlike drone. The blow struck through all pretenses because it was not sound but expectation pinned on the quality of the air, a certain shaped silence. We heard it the same as we heard the snow. Beany shivered, then went on for a while, rocking and humming, rocking and humming, a mechanical bug winding down to a stall.

Mamalou's gasping sobs (invariably surprised), rattle of the loose glass doorknob, his footsteps beating down the stairs, shuddering oak slam of the hall door. The snow. Kneeling on my pillow I watched my father, hatless on the stone steps, face buried in the crook of his arm though there was no wind.

In the alley he stood bowed beneath the shelf of tangled creeper bushes. Snow began to collect on his shoulders; then he stumbled to his car, bright as an eggplant under the streetlight, swiped peepholes clear on the windshield, and got in. He forgot to turn on the headlights; the big Packard floated off, a dim shape evaporating from our hill. Something moved at Deardorff's bedroom window, and then the lights went out.

Mamalou's tears had no power over me. They would go on to daybreak, till noon. No longer did I go with timid comfort to her bed. My father in his dark ship, swallowed up. What could compare to this? Not short skirts, not belching in catechism, not dancing goldfish on the oiled floor. These were *the times;* I was in them now, dumb as a gym shoe riding the drum of a clothes dryer.

Sudden weight around my neck, hand dragging me down. My sister, hoisting herself up with my body, one foot on the headboard, ghostly in her pale nightgown and fish eyes, blank. Now balanced on the headboard and still climbing, scraping at the glass for purchase, grip on the cornice, foot on the mullions, climbing, dead voice: "Gotta get to bed, gotta get to bed, to bed."

"Crimanees, where the heck ya go-in?"

Her eyes stared straight at mine. "Upstairs to bed," she said and tried to get a toehold in the curtain. She was so weightless, long like me, made of our father's bamboo bones. I tipped her backward easily and broke her fall by grabbing a fistful of flannel nightgown, pretended to be wrenched down myself, beside her, nearly on top of her, her sweetness, warmth—she was not quite eight to my eleven; her head still smelled of baby sweat; I wanted her to wake up. In better times she hated when I called her Rosie Rat. Stranded now by violence, softened, I rushed to be tender, to treat wounds. I whispered, "You okay, Beans?" Then, "Listen, I got an idea."

Her mouth made a chewing motion and she tried to struggle out of my encumbrance. "Let's go to church," I insisted. "We'll pray for—things." I shook her. "Want a divorce? Want Dad to marry Mrs. Rediklip?" (She was the only divorced person I knew, and she and her kids stank to heaven.) "Look, we'll go to early Mass. She'll never know we're gone." A loud sob rumbled over us from down the hall.

"Okay," Beany said brightly, smacked her lips, and still slept.

To be perfectly honest, I was afraid of the weekday earliness. Lying in bed sleepless was one thing; quite another to actually get up and perform life. I imagined my limbs moving puppetlike or not at all; even the air might be different, the way it was in space. It was like setting out into the unknown. Whatever, it wasn't real the same as lunchtime was real. I feared that a quick move, a bold stroke in that gauzy hour, could be fatal.

Just before five I shoved a pillow under Beany's head, which was down at the foot of the bed, and brought a blanket up around her, envelope-style. I slipped out of bed. Folded over the arm of our maple chair were yesterday's clothes: a quilted circular skirt, a cuffed white blouse. I dressed slowly, awkwardly. My crinolines, two of them, stood erect in the middle of the floor. I pulled on the one with the elastic waistband and the tiers of ruffled tulle. The one supposedly made of horsehair, which I always wore underneath, had a single button that came off in my hand. I quickly fixed it with a safety pin and believed I could fix anything. It felt good to be taking measures.

I got my big gray coat and wool church babushka out of the hall closet downstairs, struggled into my stadium boots. Outside, my father's tracks on the steps were nearly covered, vague print where his car had been. I lowered my head and battered into the dwindling snowfall as if it all depended on me.

Snow light and the light from the streetlamps. Shreds of dawn showing through the tattered night sky. Otherwise it was still dark.

Only five or so blocks but hard going on unshoveled walks. Manamaugh Pike nearly deserted except for Dr. Deardorff's Nash, left two feet from the curb in the trolley stop. Occasional watery glow of a second-story window through the curtain of snow starting hard again, coming large-flaked, dense, straight as pleats, as slubs on silk. It was not cold, still no wind. There was a moment as I turned onto Greeve Street and the tower of Saint Anselm loomed suddenly over the rooftops, shadowy and unreachable, and the snow streamed down, that I touched the tip of some rare knowledge, saw my foolish plowing figure fixed for all time in a snow-globe, scruffing along forever, or I was a dream or something dimly remembered, and in that split-second's reckoning, it mattered nothing that Mamalou made landscapes out of glass straws and my father was gone again.

Next to the rectory, the jagged hull of the school-under-construction, the cranes and equipment, all plastered now into a single, far-flung sculpture. If Saint Anselm's was finished by September, I would be in the first eighth-grade graduating class. I promised God on the spot to mind the nuns better than I did my teachers at Lloyd Junior High—for a price.

On the walk between the rectory and the church, the blurred dark bundle that had to be Father Gringer. Through the side door, insubstantially. A short, round priest, assistant pastor, he pressed too hard, they said. Always blessing houses. Mrs. Agnoli blew her top because he dropped the holy-water bottle under the crib and woke the baby. Full of glad tidings and congratulations, the holy-card man. Every cent he made must have gone for religious objects to be inscribed in his careful calligraphy and passed out to commemorate achievement, even the most inconsequential, honor roll and first communion, spelling bee, job promotion, childbirth.

Only a handful of worshipers, hunched grayly in their pews, coldly, because the full, generous weather was *outside* and small dismal puddles lay in the aisles, the air hung early-morning damp. The altar with its six quiet candles held just enough warmth and distant promise to make you shiver. Poinsettias from Christmas.

I clomped up the center aisle, skirt billowing out of my coat, to a pew close enough to mark my sincerity but far enough back to avoid the nuns, in their perky black bonnets, stiff across the front pew, like a single branch of watchful crows. At this hour I felt illegitimate, under-age. Maybe there was a canonical law. . .

I knelt to the statue of the Immaculate Heart, but it was really to the image of my father hiding in his sleeve,

Mamalou conducting her terrible symphony. I focused on the pink scrubbed heart, to which the Virgin pointed with hands delicate as orchids. It was chipped in several places and the bloodless white wounds made me think of the pernicious anemia my grandfather died of. I was too light-headed to pray.

Father Gringer exploding into the sanctuary as if vitality were a reasonable choice under the circumstances, the altar boys combed slick, shuffling. Deep genuflection; breezy, triumphant ascent to the altar. The only priest at Anselm's who said Mass as if he meant it, and I never understood what there was to mean. The others, mumbly and inexact of gesture, always seemed holier.

Booming organ, the gallery dripping slow *Kyries*. So small and sleepy, in fact, was the voice of the organist that the nuns in the first row must have heard her only as a buzzing in the ears. To Father Gringer, more distant still, spinning, bowing, throwing his arms out broadly, roundly melodic, she would have stirred only a perverse and mocking silence.

Everybody, everything so lifeless, drawn back, obliterated in the common grayness, but Father Gringer, golden and bejeweled, every bit as avid as a tap-dancing ten-year-old on *Ted Mack*. He gave us a holy card once and wrote on the back: *To the fine Flynn family whose hospitality is tip-tops. Thanks for the spaghetti dinner. June 1954. Sincerely in Christ, Fr. Ellis P. Gringer.* I lived in fear that he would find out, the world discover the truth about us or, worse, that nobody would ever find out and nobody save us.

Alert to the importance of attending the proceedings

closely, I tried hard to follow the missal. My finger kept faithful pace with the printed Word, but there was no calling back the wild and random mischief of the mind. Flirting with thoughts of home: (1) They come back early from a wedding because Mamalou is pie-eyed, dahlias flopping in her hair, a glob of wedding cake stuck to the seat of her dress. She chases my father around the pear tree in our yard singsonging, "Fingie chops, fingie chops." She is trying to jab her fingertips at his ribs, and he pretends to resist the tickling, tries to appear fussingly sober until he slips on the ripe pears under his feet. They wrestle on the ground laughing, tickling, oblivious, and every time they try to get up they start sliding around in the mushed fruit, keep falling back into each other's arms. Bliss, I believed, had a distinct odor: It was the smell of rotten pears. (2) Something Mamalou has said (what *was* it?) stops my father on the stairs, his narrow back no wall against her impulse, not enough left in him even to hit her, his sudden turning in to us, eyes a pink flowering of real tears. (Why did I want to cover his body when he would never have gone naked in the house, that one time of his tears more terrible than all her nights.)

Concentrate. Straighten up: Sister Patrice at catechism demonstrating the folly of three-point landings in the pews, sit-kneeling before the King. The tall, spiky one in the middle, if she knew how far afield I could go, that my mind undressed them all at the Offertory and saw—nothing, nothing but skin stretched across like doll plastic. Ashamed, I took up my rosary and remembered how she could rage against the ignorance of those who would carry rosaries to Mass.

(I took a dare once and jumped out of Janey Mc-
Call's bedroom window. I broke my leg in two places.
It hurt so much I prayed for *the times* instead; pain was
a store you shopped in. *Hosanna in excelsis.*)

At the Concentration I thumped my breast and felt
laughter bubbling up, the kind that takes you by surprise in quiet public places on the merits of some old,
otherwise forgotten joke. My father rarely meant to be
funny, and despite all that I've said and what I'm about
to say, he was the gentlest of men. I insist on that. His
gravest fault, aside from that lap-along contentment, was
a certain rashness, a penchant for the ill-considered word
or move. A Sunday morning in early June, Anselm's
window cranked open, currents of cool air gathering
humidity, halfhearted bells to the raised chalice; I am
drowsy, dimly noting the crisp crawl of a wasp across
the Vitalis-ed head of a man in front of us, and just that
quickly my father is rolling his *Sunday Visitor* into a stiff
tube, taking, in Mamalou's words, "a helluva great uncle of a swat!" The man whirls around, his entire row
turning like a skewerful of onions.

Through Him and with Him and in Him.

There was still time. I was good at Communion, could
usually feel the Host breaking down into essential graces,
giving sustenance, though sometimes I envisioned some
toothy creature feeding on me, probably because my
stomach was growling and empty. I prayed confidently
in Latin, *Agnus dei, miserere nobis,* now was the time to
get down to business.

First came the organist, light running steps from the
gallery, fast trot down the side aisle, hurry to get back

up, swallow what was dissolved and never chewed, sufficiently reflect, be ready to answer, however inaudibly,
Father Gringer's elegantly modeled *Dominus vobiscum.*
The sisters, in no hurry, but next for the propriety of
it. The rest, the common faithful, slouched, straggling
up to the rail like sleepwalkers (Beany scaling head-
boards and windows). I went last because I was a child.

The end of the line led to a place on the kneeler just
beneath the votive candles, which meant I would have
to cross in front of the nuns to return to my seat (unless I decided to thread myself into the side aisle instead and go to a different pew, but such strategies
seemed unthinkable, if not dangerous, in the context
of this covenish gathering at dawn. One bold stroke. . .)

It happened the second I stretched up toward Father Gringer's hand, a sticking in my side sharp enough
to make me draw back. Father Gringer waited for my
tongue, then laid the wafer on delicately before riffling
the air with a spin-around toward the altar, his brisk
re-ascent.

Grateful for the opportunity, I offered up the pin-
prick of pain and assumed my most pious position, eyes
closed enough to squeeze space and light into a trem-
ble, hands praying. As I passed only inches in front of
the nuns, who I imagined to be solidly impressed, I felt
on the bare skin just above the fur on my boots a sensation that might have been a coarse-haired dog brush-
ing by. Squinting down, I saw the frothy fullness of the
inner slip, the bristly horsehair I'd fixed and forgotten.
It hung a good six inches below my coat and was still
traveling. In seconds it touched my toes, the ground. I
stared stupidly ahead, walking it along the floor with

tiny, toy-soldier steps. Instinct, not strategy, pitched me
into the first pew, across the center aisle from the nuns.

I buried my burning face in trembling hands and
pretended to shut out the world for the sake of the Body
and Blood of Christ. Shame, savage and shameless,
pushed all thought of Him from my heart. I would never
emerge from the purple-stippled, swallowing depths,
never come up again. The Flynn girl who couldn't keep
her underwear on (they said that about Mrs. Rediklip),
what could you expect, coming from *that* family, how
they carry on nights. . . . The soft upper band of the
horsehair clung precariously, ignominiously under the
lower curve of my buttocks.

When finally I peeked an eye through parted fingers, an altar boy was extinguishing the high Mass candles. The flat white light of winter morning snuffed the
yellow glow. The nun's pew was empty. Father Gringer
hocking smoker's phlegm in the sacristy, sound of heavy
doors settling against their jambs, whispered greetings
in the vestibule, a purely secular guffaw. Solid sides of
a school morning bricking up, ordinary air smelling of
fresh snow, the world handed back to itself. How sad I
wanted to be!

And could not. I stayed for a while, holding the
wretched horsehair business against the upheavals of the
night before. I seemed unable to work up a decent pang
for either disaster and refused to choose between them.
I had ruined Communion and betrayed my parents, sold
out for the luxury of wholehearted humiliation. De-
tached and dry, I understood the sweep of my guilt and
accepted full responsibility for the dissolutions to come.
I offered the whole works up for my grandfather's soul

and felt lightened, the way I did the day he finally died.

When I was certain the church was deserted, I jiggled the horsehair out from between my knees and the kneeler. Then I sneaked my fingers under the waistband of my skirt, fishing first for the top of the slip, then for the safety pin. Hitching and twisting, I eventually had enough of the horsehair in hand to work with. For the second time that day I made my homely repairs, but this time I was not fooled: Nothing ever got fixed for good. I hurried to get out to the snow and the morning, for they were suddenly tender beyond the pull of heaven, more fragile, faster than birds. The snow had stopped and there was a light wind, by turns stirring and chilling the hope that maybe by now my father was caught in a glorious grinding and sparking of tires halfway up our accursed hill.

Ode to the Big School

Many years ago my kid brother used ro recite a kindergarten rhyme with such irresistible solemnity that we would nearly cannibalize him with kisses. It began, "Oh, to the big school I shall go and learn all the things I want to know." Blaise died instantly in a Viet Cong mortar blast that left him unscratched but dead nonetheless. Dead of something they'd called "concussive insult." Just as cleanly, my son was born that same year, the event complicated by nothing more than the predictable resonances then attending a birth out of wedlock. The boisterous rituals of affection I'd performed for Blaise—the great well of emotion still pumping love, like a severed heart—I immediately transferred to tiny Wally. As if by specific bequest. Often I'd forget and call him Blaise. Except for their pale eyes, they bore little resemblance to each other; it was only the quality of my joy that was the same. In bursts of exuberant buffoonery I used Blaise's song to commemorate Wally's passage into first grade, junior high, then high school. One day in the fall of his senior year he and I were on our way down to a certain formidable old eastern university. Wally was behind the wheel and we'd both been acting silly, from nerves and hopelessness. In a trembly falsetto he started to trill: "Oh, to the big school I shall go. . . ."

"Likely story," I said, trying to laugh past the sudden lump in my throat.

The truth was neither of us expected any more of this outing than a day off. This was a school of brahmins and bluestockings; we had no family roots sunk in that campus, no tradition to confirm him, not much money. From the age of seven he had lived among the children of dairymen and alfalfa farmers; he loved gravy bread and was likely to say "them," as in "them apples," and unless he made it a point not to, "you'uns" and "chimley." We were only making the trip because of the wrestling coach, who was, at the moment, only moderately interested. Mr. Kokoruda had phoned and said he'd like to show us around the school. Then later, should Wally become a state champion or something, the wishy-washiness would rinse away, leaving a rock-solid, 24-carat commitment that pretended to have been always apparent, as if admission had been, from the start, a foregone conclusion. We have not lived in the country so long as to be blind to the remorseless logic of such things.

"You shoulda worn your bowling shirt, Mom." I don't know how to bowl but I got the point. "You shoulda worn your high-water pants—with clodhoppers," I said.

"Saaaay, Kokoruda," Wally said, affecting a precise down-home drawl, "nice place you got here. Indoor plumbing, real window glass, store-bought soap. Gaw-leeee!"

We went on like that for a while, how we were going to pick our teeth and scratch like terriers, pull Spam sandwiches and half-pints of milk out of our pockets at lunchtime. We were laughing so hard that I made Wally pull off the road into a fast-food place. Even though it was nine o'clock in the morning I bought him a bag of chili dogs and cole slaw, a strawberry milkshake. At home he was known by his appetite; kids gathered to cheer him on in the school cafeteria, offer the limas from their succotash, leftover macaroni salad. Often I caught myself brightly listing the numbers and size of his portions as if they were academic degrees. I let him go back for two slices of pizza: Soon enough the rigors of wrestling season would lash him to a long and hungry winter, soon enough.

On the last leg of the trip we abandoned the self-parody for a sort of indignation that was at least half in earnest. "Wally," I said, "we are not going to slaver."

He said, "Yeah!" with stagy determination. "And we're not going to grovel either—Great place, Kokoruda, but I had something a little less, uh, prognathous, in mind." This was part of the problem, of course. He had no idea what *prognathous* meant.

"Gosh, coach." I squeezed my voice into a ball of mealymouthed apology. "If only your initials weren't P.U."

"I got other offers, Kokoruda. Ever hear of Sherman Herman Institute of Technology? Huh? Huh? Didja? Put that in your gym shoe, Kokoruda." He said it all in a wonderfully exaggerated Pennsylvania Dutch inflection that made him sound knee-deep in cow-pies. Over the years he'd managed to acquire as well the unmistakable look of the country-bred, a thatchy-headed gawkiness and lumpish candor that could move or mortify me depending on the state of my mental health at the time. But there was also something else, a quality

91

clearly evocative of the school in question: another face—subtler, smoother, colder, a more elegant profile—waiting to be chiseled from the crude form of the laughing, mugging original. I went suddenly soft with knowing he would indeed get in: love-soft, soft as the edges of unaccountable sadness.

These prophetic flashes are not as rare as they are temporary. As soon as I saw the spires, the gray stone walls breathing out of that long, redoubtable history, I knew once again we didn't stand a chance. *We, people like us,* whoever we were, whatever that meant. Eyes that peered out of the muck of such meditations saw that Wally's lapels were too wide. Was the blue of his jacket the one socially inexcusable blue? Lord, he must have picked his face last night.

We asked for directions to the new gym. Bright-faced, courteous students in Icelandic wool sweaters and down-filled vests replied in sterling tones, aggressively forthright. They sent us to the infirmary, then to the kosher cafeteria, the crewing lake. Wally stopped the car in the middle of the roadway and turned to me. "What are we doing here?" he asked softly. "Zis world wiseass headquarters or what?" His shoulders slumped, his blue eyes light as tap water almost; hurt bleaches them that way, and I was reminded of the time Mama and I tried to get Blaise's boots on. I was ten and he was a woebegone five in a neighborhood thick with socially exclusive seven-year-olds. One slushy Saturday in December, two of these children—a boy and a girl—came to the door and, incredibly, asked if Blaise could come out. Mama gave them grateful—no, obsequious—cookies and asked them to wait in the hall while we rushed about

gathering all his winter gear. We threw a hastily pack-
aged, ecstatic Blaise on the sofa and started to jam the
wrong feet into red rubber boots. There were giggles
and then I heard the front door slam. When I went out
to check, the children were gone. I spotted them a half-
block down the street, alternately running and stopping to look back and laugh. In bedroom slippers and
pedal pushers, we took off after them, chased them all
over the block through soggy backyards and roadside
mounds of soft, soiled snow. We hollered after them.
"Snots!" I cried. "Stinkers!" from Mama. Pin worms!
Pissants! I felt the same murderous surge on the campus that day, part of me up and thumping after the
clear-eyed princes and princesses. I, ferocious, jagged-
edged, a whorl of applied malevolence. The rancor
made my teeth hurt.

Somebody behind us honked and Wally started slowly
forward again. "Oh, Bogus!" he said. "Let's just drive
around till the freakin gym shows up. I'll know it when
I see it. Looks like a humungous white armadillo, I read
somewhere."

I expected Mr. Kokoruda to be in warm-ups or running shorts, but we found him behind a gray metal desk
in a small uncluttered office. Harris tweed sports jacket,
knit tie, pale-yellow shirt. Younger than myself. Blaise,
had he lived, would be about this man's age. And Wally
was very nearly the exact age Blaise would be forever.
Absurdly, this struck me as some kind of portentous
mystical connection. I wanted to stop and reflect on the
numerology. Multiply by the day of the week, divide by
the number of combs in my purse. Lost, one invariably
looks for signs. But he was advancing now with his hand

extended. His voice was clean, voluble, made me think of real estate men or faith healers. "Good to see ya folks. Any trouble on the way down? Good, good, great to see ya."

We all sat down and everything went dead-still for several seconds. Then he said, "Soooo. So you think you'd like to wrestle for us?" Which was fine except that he was looking at me when he said that. Not looking exactly but fixing on my coat sleeve, more or less.

I shot Wally a nudging glance and he said, "Uh, me? Sure, well, uh, sure."

Kokoruda rose abruptly out of his chair and came around to the front of the desk. He straddled first one corner, then moved to the other, sat and clasped his hands around his knee. He had small confetti-green eyes in a large pleasant face, a deeply cleft chin, square chest, short legs. He leaned forward: "Let me say this to ya, Wall. I think we have what you're looking for—correct me if I'm wrong. Super undergraduate program. Solid tradition. Status," he added importantly, raising an index finger. "First-rate facilities—did ya see Beekwell yet? Super faculty—these are the fellas wrote the textbooks. Buncha super guys on the team." He used fastidious little tugs on his fingertips like commas. "Small college atmosphere. . ." He swallowed and then it seemed he just shut down, his face a plaster life-mask hardening around a nascent ache.

Smiling shyly into his lap, Wally said, "Uh-huh." All those reckless speeches on the way down and the best he could do here was sure, well, uh-huh. That must have been about the time I started with the nonstop nattering. I played words like desperate pinballs, sent them

skittering slapdash against Wally's exasperating dumbness and all the other odd, untimely silences in the room.

"We noticed a lot of great old trees," I said. "Didn't
we, Wally? Must be lots of shade here in the summer.
I hate to see campus buildings sitting out like orphans
in the middle of a cornfield. I'm thinking of a school
back home. Leitel Hall is so far out the kids call it Lei-
tel-house-on-the-prairie."

He pulled at his lips. "Yes, we have a more, uh, es-
tablished, uh, look here." I blathered on something about
how the very quality of the air seemed to change once
we'd passed through the university gates. Denser, com-
pacted, I said; the molecules seemed jammed together
like the books on library shelves.

He nodded, staring at my sleeve again. "I guess that's
what we call upper atmosphere." He laughed weakly.

"Oh, no," I said, unable to stop myself, as if I were
being paid and paid well to drive home feckless points.
"In that case the air would be thinner, wouldn't it?"

"Look," he said, "I'd like to show you around, take
you to lunch." He said this flatly. I had a sense, then,
of his body going heavy, inert, resistant, of his trapped
eyes asking us to go away forever. Wally rose awkwardly, a gangly kid, suddenly too large for the room.
Although not quite sure what protocol had been
breached, I was desperate for redemption. I looked
around. "Oh, my," I said. "Do they belong to you?" I
indicated a folding double frame: two children, a fair-
haired boy of perhaps four, a baby girl with a wobbly,
bonneted head.

"Marcus and Mary Beth," he said, drawing a ragged
breath.

"They're quite beautiful," I cooed. "Lovely children."

"They look more like their mother," he said dully. Another gilt frame lay face down in the middle of the desk. He walked over and snapped off the lights with an abruptness that might have betokened reproach or a mere professional crispness.

Beekwell gym did not give off the usual seep of decades of sweat and dirty socks distilled to a palpable organic presence. If anything it smelled like an empty cathedral, of immutable laws and chilly candlesticks. We stood bowed beneath the double-domed ceiling: the massiveness, the quietude, the settled dimness. "Holy Bogus!" Wally whispered. In the distant heart of the interior a single workman, coolly sacerdotal, moved soundlessly along the indoor track on his knees, rubbing something on the smooth green baize. "We hold all our matches here now," Mr. Kokoruda said softly, proudly. But I couldn't quite evoke the motion, the flesh, or the secular thunder.

Then we went to the library, the student pub, the older, gamier gym. Either Kokoruda led us around at a hectic pace, explaining nothing, or dawdled unaccountably, mumbling sporadic jolts of data about the architecture or wealthy alumni donors. Wally's face had become a block of frozen attention. When Kokoruda told us how he'd had to finagle admissions one year to get a wrestler in with 520 verbals, Wally's chin dropped. "What's yours, by the way?" he asked. "Six-ten, twenty?"

"Uh, any weak spots in your lineup?" I quickly interrupted.

"We could use a coupla good lightweights," he said.

It was mild for November, but the trees were nearly

bare. In one of the quadrangles, students chased one another with long cardboard carpet rolls and played coed football. There was an uncertainty about the sunlight, and their playfulness had a hard, hysterical edge to it, a sense of unwitting urgency that pulled me in. For just that instant I forgot it was Wally, not I, who was seventeen and shopping for a college. My heart grew tender and wild as a teenager's, swollen with longing, a sweet youthful vehemence against the shortening days. Oh, the heat under the sleeves of their sweaters, the hard animal teeth, time so tight and yet so soft around them, and later there would be white milk and *Swann's Way* and the hiss of dormitory radiators. When the moment lapsed, it came as a shock to me that I wouldn't be coming back next year to play touch football and read Proust, that nobody would believe me if I said I was still a child.

Mr. Kokoruda took us to a bright-yellow faculty lounge for lunch. Wally selected, with infuriatingly spurious delicacy, a bowl of chowder and a small salad. He gave me an icy look when I asked for a double cheeseburger, french fries, and a piece of chipolata pie. "I rushed off without breakfast," I hastily explained to Mr. Kokoruda as we stood waiting in the cafeteria line. He bent toward me, semi-intimately. "Eat up," he whispered. "This is a rich school." He smelled faintly of Palmolive soap.

We were on the fourth floor, our table near the window. The frail haze of autumnal light brought the color of the buildings up to a nacreous, dreamy violet. On three sides campus boundaries were visible: that contrived, closed world, timeless as a churchyard. It made my throat ache. Next to me, my son, sitting mute as a gargoyle, blew on prissy spoonfuls of cold soup.

"You didn't tell me about those S.A.T.'s, Wall?" Mr. Kokoruda was having a strawberry yogurt and coffee.

Wally cleared his throat. "Seven-ten math. Five-ten verbals."

The coach hesitated. "Math is fine," he said. "Fine." He raised a spoonful of yogurt almost to his mouth, then buried it again in the cup. A shiver passed across his shoulders. At the same time a massive fist of clouds poised over the chapel spire grabbed away the light and, moments later, flung it down again. After a very long time Wally looked up and asked, "You expecting a winning season?"

"Decent," Kokoruda said. He started to run down the weight classes. He kept losing his train of thought. He'd go silent and start over. "We haven't had an NCAA champ since Musselman, you know." There was a slow, cumbersome quality about his voice, a lassitude inexplicable in terms of years between championships.

Grimacing sympathetically, Wally quickly set himself to spearing the last bits of onion out of his bowl. I was aware of sucking in great wads of silence, chewing them up and spitting out words: an automatic processor of dullness and discomfiture. "Musselman?" I said. "A wrestler named Musselman?"

"Huh? Oh, oh but that's M-u-s-s-e-l. . ."

"Stiiiiil!" I said. "It's sort of a hobby I have."

"What is?"

"Names. Collecting outrageous ones or ones that're particularly apt."

He looked at me blankly, uncomprehending, his large

white face inaccessible as the surface of the moon. I rushed on. "Ever hear of Judge Learned Hand or Dr. E. Z. Needles?"

He shook his head unblinkingly. The possibility that he thought me insufferable or bizarre had no effect at this point but to goad me on. Or perhaps I was caught in one of those fateful currents whereby we keep drowning a blunder beneath successive waves of increasingly greater ones. I went on. "The best one I ever encountered personally was a boy my brother knew in grade school. His name was Positive Wassermann Pickett—his given name, I swear."

Seconds passed. He finally made a mirthless sound and repeated the word *Pickett*. "Well, no," I said. "I meant the Positive Wassermann part."

He stared at me. I said, "Named after the Wassermann test of course." I waited. I was never good at games that require long-range planning. Only now was I beginning to see where I was headed. "You know. . ." I began. "You know what that is, don't you?"

Barely perceptibly his head moved on a bull-like neck. No, it was saying. He continued to stare and if I thought I could trust my judgment at that point, I would have said he looked bewildered—frightened even. I had a sense of his swelling to a critical, warning fullness and could not bear to watch his face. This time I fixed on *his* sleeve. I said, "A Wassermann's the blood test required by law when you get married." I looked up quickly and because his expression had not changed, I added miserably, "For syphilis."

He nodded, his eyes distant and dazed. Then Wally pushed away from the table, asking haltingly after the

99

men's room. I excused myself with equal awkwardness. When I returned, Mr. Kokoruda was not in his seat. I found him in the hallway, facing out a window. I came up to within several feet of him, glanced up, and from an oblique angle, saw the slick white crescent curve of his cheek. I backed quietly away and went back into the cafeteria to wait for Wally.

Later Kokoruda told us to meet him back at Beekwell in an hour. He was standing outside the building when we got there. He was warm and hearty, salesmanlike again. He shook Wally's hand and told him to bring up the verbals and apply as soon as possible. "I'll be glad to go to bat for you when the time comes," he said.

It was months before either of us could bring ourselves to talk about that day. Wally went ahead and mailed his application because, as it turned out, he really had been smitten, and longing is so easily confused with likelihood. He worried his verbals up another thirty points and, lacking the more orthodox whiz-kid wonderments, wrote a disarming essay about seeing the world from his pogo stick.

One night in the middle of wrestling season, when he was at his purest and hungriest, sunken-cheeked and spiritually isolate, he started to sob uncontrollably as he carried in an armload of firewood. "I was thinking about that time with Kokoruda. When he found out about my verbals. He hated us. He couldn't wait for us to leave. Remember how funny he got, quiet or bored. Spaced out."

"Yes," I said.

"He was so disappointed in me." He dropped his kindling into the holder and wiped his eyes, eyes fading to tinted tap water, shimmering. "He was just wasting his time."

"It wasn't you at all. I'm sure of it." I led him to the sofa. "Except you talked too damn much."

"I felt so dumb."

"Me too. I love you, Blaise," I said. For now it was sadness that confused me. But I was glad, too—grateful for this moment—for I did not know what catastrophe, what disappointment, what grief before he'd let me hold the bony length of him again.

Even side doors lead to the main arena. Wally didn't become a state champion, but he did finish third and accomplished with a double arm-bar and a cradle what a host of valedictorians couldn't do with a thousand dozen A's. Days after his letter of acceptance arrived he ran around the house saying, "Oh, to the big school, oh, to the big school I shall go. Whooooo!" For graduation I gave him his uncle's Miraculous Medal, which had failed, of course, to protect him. Perhaps it would know more about magic this time around. And I gave him a poem. I called it "Ode to the Big School," but I couldn't think of anything to say so I left the paper blank, hoping he'd think the blankness conceptual or compelling.

There was a lot I didn't say that year. I never told him, for instance, that when I walked away from Mr. Kokoruda in the hall outside the cafeteria, it was because I finally had sense enough to know when to stop. There had been a lick of wetness under the coach's cheekbone, what remained perhaps after hastily swiped tears; I might even have seen the tears, then watched him erase them. Whatever, I didn't tell Wally—I don't know—out of gratitude to the man for rescuing me from the moil of self-rebuke; out of some sense of partnership in loss. I surely owed him that much of silence for barging in on whatever his grief, and stomping around all day in clodhoppers.

But also, and probably mostly, I really was still a child—or maybe just an unmarried woman—with winter on my hands and sweet, warm secrets.

When the time came for Wally to leave, I relinquished him with surprising grace, such willingness having perhaps matured unawares, like a seventeen-year locust of the heart. But Mr. Kokoruda was not so easy to let go. How slickly, how conveniently I had grown attached—stuck fast at nearly every point where we had touched: that moment of intimate witnessing, that yearlong loyalty against my own. I'd invented a hundred names and countless villains for his sorrow. Hadn't even his age meant something to me? Hadn't he whispered to me in the cafeteria line? Unloosed, one looks for connections.

In soft putty-colored sweaters, Wally comes back from time to time. He speaks rather warmly of Nietzsche, snidely of Sartre. "Wow," he says, looking around, "home feels weird, like going to Grandma's for Christmas." Of course, I still make all his favorite things. He looks forward to the unstinting mounds of breaded veal and lemon slices, chive potatoes, banana bread. I set full gallons before him and then, when he is wholly engaged, least open to innuendo, I lean forward, sliding plates of flummery or butter creams, putting the question to him slyly, haltingly as an inquiring ex-wife. "And Kokoruda?" I ask. "Is he well? Is he happy?"

The Barlip Run

Every Sunday morning Dolbin Cee opened his eyes and adjudged, by the insolence of the light, the hour and his chances of getting a *New York Times*. From seven to eight-thirty, reasonable; tapering off past nine; nil after ten. On some occasions he awakened Mrs. Cee, whose first activity of the day was to struggle violently against her own visions, whose first words were always: "Where am I?" So slowly did conviction return to her puzzled, sorrowing face that, more often than not, Dolbin let her sleep and drove the five miles to Barlip alone.

Though no longer a stranger to the area, he could still be mildly tickled by the drolleries of the landscape: how the roads skinned the corners of farmhouses and barns: the patient, foolish heads of dairy cows trapped in the low fences; Amish buggies, ubiquitous and imperturbable; the fields lying cozy and smug as quilts; black-bumper Mennonite boys sneaking smokes behind the springhouse; the Blue Mountains circling, sharp or hazy, teasing, so that the horizon was sometimes bestowed and sometimes revoked. And Dolbin below, leery of the hour, driving a mite fast around those jutting porches, waving a bit too vigorously to the deadpan farmers.

He took a kind of childish delight in striding into Bouch's of a Sunday, in greeting the good ol' boys

crowding the ice-cream freezer, who conversed laconi-
cally in Pennsylvania Dutch and sometimes nodded
tersely back; in claiming a crisp *Times* from the miserly
stack. The heft of it in his hand, the fleshy way it slapped
the counter. It was his wont, then, to lay a conciliatory
Kretztown Eagle on top.

Sometimes it was Jakey who waited on him. He had
a round bashful face, a blushing frontal baldness, and
always something awkwardly, hokily amusing to say
about the weather or the headlines. Otherwise it was
necessary to deal with one of his two stout sisters with
their pecking eyes and underbites gaping naked as grain
scoops. They glowered when he had no pennies,
drummed impatient fingers if he didn't move quickly
enough away from the counter. Occasionally, having
arrived to find the supply sold out, he might, in a moment of sheer devilishness, ask one or the other, "Where
are *The New York Times* today?" just to hear her snarl,
"Don't ya have eyes, Mister? They're all!" Asking aloud
also published his tastes, his uniqueness here among the
locals, who were bound to suspect in him anyhow some
hidden superiority, if only in the way his past could
endlessly, craftily, re-form outside the limits of their
knowledge of him and set itself up smart as new nails,
undulled by *their* definitions, *their* dailiness, and out of
the same mythic pocket of cunning continue to elude
their hard curiosity. This he half believed and half re-
jected; in his heart he was afraid of them.

In time he would surely have made his chary peace
with this weekly exercise in uncertainty and subjuga-
tion had he not happened to notice one Sunday a cache
of tellingly substantial newspapers on a shelf behind the

counter: "And what might those be?" he asked the one called Elvina.

That he should even ask! She stared at him in disbelief, her lower lip hanging slack and wet over the savage jaw, her chest one straining roundness. But when it became clear that he would stand there stupid with wonder, perhaps indefinitely, she muttered, "Them are put back for the reklers."

He nodded thoughtfully and imagined his eyes staring helpless, uncomplaining as the trapped cow's. Then at the first opportunity, he drew the gentle-faced Jakey aside and quietly requested the same privilege for himself.

"Sure thing!" the man replied. "Are you going back where you came from?"

"You mean am I going back the way I came, don't you?"

Jakey shrugged and smiled shyly, then made his customary muggy-weather joke, which was to advise Dolbin to button up his coat on the way out.

There followed from that day a period of unprecedented harmony and contentment. Dolbin and Mrs. Cee slept late Sundays and she seemed not so startled now by the familiar, the unarguable rhythms, and together they decided to make love or not, clip each other's toenails or not, close the windows or not. In the kitchen they took their time, he slicing sunlit bananas and she apricots into silver bowls of sugared cream. And Mrs. Cee might cut asters for the breakfast table from a garden kept remarkably weed-free by Dolbin with newspaper mulch layered over with pine needles and old leaves. (Dolbin is confounded by weeds, their ravening good health, their relentless militancy against his own interpretations.) And then again she might not.

Together they made the Barlip run, stopping off at Boopie's for a local cantaloupe, fetching raw milk from one of those houses bumping the road. Smiling benevolently, they waited for ducklings to cross in front of them; they gathered grasses and pods for winter bouquets, each time delaying by a little—giddily testing— the moment when they would appear in Bouch's doorway, flushed with faith yet always freshly gladdened, edified, grateful, even somehow surprised to find that single, guarded *New York Sunday Times* waiting whole and unappropriated on the back shelf.

At home Dolbin carefully removed the crossword puzzle and turned over the magazine to Mrs. Cee, who believed the articles too honor-bright, the ads ludicrously low-key and patient, the recipes downright malicious (2 madder-wort roots! 36 fresh rose petals!) But she felt comfortable in the mellow aura of Russell Baker's seasoned fussiness and enjoyed watching Safire make nitpickery respectable. After the rigors of the puzzle Dolbin always napped for an hour, then read the *Book Review*, timidly, hoping not to find the novel he would one day write.

Then Mrs. Cee gathered the papers and laid them on the mulching pile in the basement. Because of the thickness of its sections, the *Times* was ideal for the garden; only a bull thistle could drill up through thirty-six pages in a single season.

If Dolbin, whose self-perceptions often came in metaphorical flashes, could have viewed his life as a postage stamp—the smoothly affixed and precisely ticketed thing that it was—he would also have seen the tiny irksome bubble under the seal: this a ballooning up out of the vague unease stirred in him by Mrs. Cee's hobby. Not that there was anything patently wrong with photographing tractor-trailers—exactly (he had checked with all the quotable authorities), but some things held their infelicities close, where you couldn't get a handle or a good look, and despite his repeated admonitions he often caught her poring over the enlargements when she thought he was asleep.

In August, Mrs. Cee began to angle for a "scoot up to the Green Mountains," where the air was cool and piney, the accents "breezier." A change of pace, she said, maple syrup and cheddar cheese, and not once did she mention that stretch of mountain road where Dolbin knew she liked to stand and catch the rigs nosing menacingly over the crest, rearing up hot out of the deep, soft, cool moss of the mountain.

Of course Dolbin confronted her immediately. She quoted a passage from a little-known apologist of rational psycho-energetics which was quite lengthy and seemed to posit a presence in the world of something called metaflow particles, to all of which Dolbin had no prepared rebuttal, and so reluctantly *(reluctantly,* he would later emphasize) he agreed to go.

They rented a quiet, porchy place not far from the Appalachian Trail, and though Mrs. Cee tried to stay put, leaving only for nature walks with Dolbin, hikes into the village for groceries, he sensed her restlessness, the ineluctability of it all. And no sooner had he thought it than, as if propelled by his doom-swearing, they found themselves racing along the mountain road to that very spot where Mrs. Cee would pull over and, heart-thumping, breathless, alarmingly rapt, await the sudden, brutal thrust over the top.

It was this period that produced her finest prints: an early teal-blue Maxidyne, a vintage Diamond T, twin powder-pink Road Commanders, dogwood-stenciled; and on the very last day, heaving into sight, rapacious as a warlord, studded like an uptown dude, the outlaw Peterbilt Westcoaster flashing full custom chrome—blunt nose, rakish cab, yellow-orange pulsant lightning on metallic blue, double air-intakes, smoke belching out of twin polished-chrome exhausts. She even got an angle shot of the tandem-axle rear end as it began the downhill plunge, trembling the pines toward Rutland.

Dolbin seethed and fretted in private and kept up a public nonchalance lest their activities be found out and they be thought, at best, an interesting couple; at worst, well, he couldn't think what. He'd crouch in the shadows by the side of the road until Mrs. Cee was satisfied, and once, as he relieved himself deep in the brush, a single hiker, a boy with soft, defenseless eyes, accosted him and said, pleasantly enough: "I came to the woods to live deliberately and now I can't remember what I had in mind."

Dolbin said, yes, something was bothering him as well, but he couldn't quite put his finger on it.

It wasn't until the very second the Cees set foot inside Bouch's that the realization struck, stunningly: Two Sundays' worth of "reserveds" had neither been claimed by him nor proper notice given. He tugged at Mrs. Cee's sleeve. "Wait here," he said, squeezing her arm reassuringly. Brusque, businesslike as a supermarket manager, he hastened to the counter. To the sister called Merce he said, "Hello, we're back." And when she seemed disinclined to rescue him with a reply, he added brightly, "Lovely place, New England, this time of year."

Fixing him with a baneful stare, she stood there with her roots deep in the county, unbudging, culturally unimpeachable. She cast an impatient eye toward her sister, as if beckoning for a prearranged assist.

"I know I should have called," he said, his voice less confident, groping for the right tone. "We'll take the papers now, of course."

The two women merged their bulk into one great bunching plasticity, barrier to all his certainties, his most reliable retreats and reductions; he could see nothing now, not even the Sanitas-covered shelf that always held the earmarked, protected *Times.*

"Of course!" mocked Elvina. "Well, ya can't have them. I throwed them ott."

"We throwed them ott," Merce asseverated. She shot her jaw, challenging him.

"You threw them out," he said. A humble declarative.

"Well, did ya think we keep stale news around here forever? I wanted to run a D and B on you and Viney here says, what fer dumb, ya have to take some chances in this world. So we take a gamble and what d'ya think? Round ya come wise as ya please—*Lovely place this time of year!* Question our methods, correct our English. *What? You dumb Dutch packrats don't hang on to things forever? How indecorous of you. Heeva havvus!*"

"What's a *heeva havva?*"

A dapper little man, fretful as a footnote, came bussing forward. He poked Dolbin's arm and called for his ear. "Don't say it so dang loud," he whispered. The *heeva havva* goes round from farm to farm in the breeding season. He's the fella that guides the bull's pizzle. A chawbacon; the quintessential clod."

Each time the Cees recounted the story, Dolbin swore the Bouches really had said *indecorous* and *heeva havvas*, and Mrs. Cee confirmed it; also that the entire obloquy had been delivered in perfect, rehearsed unison, matched bulldog faces baring stained lower dentures at him.

By this time, Mrs. Cee had sidled up and hooked his arm protectively. The local boys didn't seem to bother much, and down by the front door Jakey stood humming quietly into a corner.

"Coupla pikers," Elvina spat. For a second the two bodies drew apart and Dolbin breathed that slippage of free space before their shoulders welded up the seam and closed him off.

"Hold on here. . ." he began and stumbled. Each woman wore a crisp cotton housedress in a bright floral print and a bib apron of the same fabric as the other's dress. Although he had first thought the sisters nearly interchangeable, he now noticed Elvina's larger face, her fuller head of frizzed pewter-colored hair. Her arms were splotchy and sausagelike in contrast to Merce, whose flesh swung like wide satin sleeves from armpit to elbow.

"We'll be happy to pay for those copies," offered Mrs. Cee into the gap opened by Dolbin's hesitation.

"Oh, no, we will not!" shot Dolbin. "Now I'm getting darn good and mad. Ladies," he said, drawing himself up, *"Beautiferous* ladies, you just lost yourself a couple of customers." From behind—a man waiting to pay for his *Eagle* perhaps—a voice distinctly said, "Somebody had to tell them."

Dolbin, of course, began to wish almost immediately that it had been somebody else. As Mrs. Cee said on the way home, "Now what do we do?" Where would they get any Sunday paper at all now that he'd reacted so precipitously to what was essentially a muggy-weather snit. "Dog days, Dolbin," she added.

"We'll manage," he said unconvincingly.

In the beginning he managed to manage with little difficulty. A mood of defiance woke him early Sundays and fueled the thirty-five-mile drive to Kretztown, where he could choose from among a half-dozen shops, each stocking a civilized supply of Sunday *Times* and none harboring anything so intransigent and ferocious as the Bouch sisters. He was not, however, above exaggerating the attendant hardships so as to infuse Mrs. Cee sufficiently with the folly of her wrongheadedness— which complaints served only, in the end, to stimulate reality. The trip *did* become burdensome; occasionally they overslept and even Kretztown ran out of the *Times* eventually, a development that would send them home tense and bitter and furious with a people whose houses didn't know enough to keep off the road, whose air smelled of warm grassy milk and manure, whose cows crumpled in full sun, lumpy and dumb as onion bags, who had no tongue but the thick one that beat all words level with the *heeva havva's* sympathetic grunt. And if the situation were not already oppressive enough, Mrs. Cee had to add a kind of ironic depth: She began to carry a camera on these trips, and Dolbin, increasingly powerless against these mounting perversities, silently outraged and trembling, would allow himself to be coaxed off the highway at certain predetermined spots, and there be made to lie in wait like a bushwhacker.

In the winter, of course, road conditions further complicated the problem. Then with the first flush of warm weather, the gas crunch. The trip raised, by turns, practical questions and moral ones involving American greed and world poverty. The Kretztown run became so fraught with ethical contingencies and philosophical traps that by the time Dolbin finished grappling with the issues, he was too tired or it was too late to go. When the shortage eased, Mrs. Cee objected to the higher costs left in its wake. Was the *Times* worth the four dollars in gas, plus its own rising price (fifty cents extra in the "suburbs")? Plus wear and tear on the car.

On this question Dolbin was tearfully vehement. Such things could not be measured in terms of dollars and cents (as if by clinging to a loyalty, he could maintain a tie). A new dissatisfaction had taken hold of his life, a malaise unexplainable in purely pragmatic terms. He longed not after convenience and favors or a better deal, but after a condition that had once marked him, outside of which he felt nameless and unanointed; a gratuitous ease that had been not merely an absence of hardship but a perfect intellectual location, a safe harbor.

He grew morose. He muddled through the motions of his daily existence, confused and slightly drunk with grief. In his garden, he moved slowly, tugging halfheartedly at sassy new lamb's-quarters and wild garlic, often tearing them off high above the roots. He would awaken in the middle of the night rawly certain, terrified, that a specific screwdriver or garden rake was missing, and he would have to get up and search the house until it was found. Mrs. Cee made him herbal teas and gave him vitamin E for his nerves. In a burst of tearful remorse she offered to burn her entire collection of 8 × 10 polychromes. "Well, okay," he said weakly. "Could you mebbe get me a dish of vanilla ice cream with wet walnuts and raspberry jam?"

Then one spring day, about the time when he would ordinarily have been setting out his ageratums, he read in a magazine that he alone was In Charge of His Own Life. He thumped his forehead and laughed, marveling at the hearty simplicity of it.

He began his charge-taking phase by paying a kid from down the road to ride along on the trip to Barlip. While he hunkered down in the car, the kid entered Bouch's and like some privileged nabob, Dolbin thought resentfully, emerged in minutes holding the prize. But Dolbin worried lest the Bouch sisters, suspecting this large, sleepy-eyed, shuffling country boy, demand proof of his reading tastes. He determined that if someone were to stand on the roof of the long, low building, he, Dolbin, could be readily seen. Or what if they simply followed the boy outside and caught Dolbin coiled up in the back seat? How his heart pounded and he was not getting any younger. Further, the boy grew tired of the game and finally said he'd rather sleep late on Sundays.

As the weeks passed, his obsession flared out of control. He wanted no other *Times* but theirs. He disguised himself as Mrs. Cee until he realized they might think he'd put her up to it. Sometimes he dressed in the damask robes of an Eastern Rite archbishop and stroked a scholarly gray beard. He showed up in blackface or swathed in bandages. But always it seemed they watched him with titillated eyes, and once when he came as a potato-brown gypsy, stomping and singing, scarved and glittery, they cursed at him and drove him out with brand-new brooms. There was also the ever-present danger that one of those arms—a soft flapping one or a dimpled tubular one—would shoot out from behind the cash register to test a breast or moustache.

In desperation he dropped them a note saying he was a new paraplegic in the area and couldn't handle their front stoop. If they would be so kind as to leave a copy of *The New York Sunday Times* on the curb, he would gladly remit by mail. But when he drove by the following Sunday morning the sidewalk lay in the sun like a bone-white beach, irreconcilably desolate and bereft.

Even as he contrived to defraud the Bouches of their rightful comeuppance, he mistrusted his success; the newspapers he obtained by such means were like words of love extracted by cajolery or duress. He could not forget the sugared cream Sundays, the languorous, idyllic drives. The longings raked his sleep and stopped him dead at work. He turned sullen and reclusive; the weeds grew tall and woody as rake handles. He could barely stand the sight of Mrs. Cee, who—having burned her photographs (except for the double-stacked Peterbilt), cut her hair, sworn indifference to the laid-back style of the new-model Road Commander—had run out of amends. One day he looked in the mirror and said,

I have grown from a carnivorous but kindly, moderately bookish parlor liberal with conservative suspicions to a lead-hearted, sump-eyed, savage wanderer outside the pale.

That evening he went to Mrs. Cee and, in a voice made rich with irony and dark moods, asked her this: "Do we think that by exacting our benefactions one at a time, we might compile a heaven?" For the first time in months they made love. They talked quietly in bed and agreed that he would leave off his useless strategies and go humbly back to Barlip—needful—naked of all but his lingering tristesse.

For the occasion of his nakedness he chose to dress in white: deck pants, buckskin shoes, a tennis shirt with a white monogram. When he got to Bouch's they appeared to be waiting for him and looked neither surprised nor victorious. The good ol' boys stopped talking and silently took seats on the lid of the ice-cream freezer; browsers set aside their Pocket Books. Serenely resigned, Dolbin watched Elvina and Merce beckon their soft, bald brother, who was taking a tin of Borkhum Riff off the shelf. *"Now*, Chakey," urged Merce. The women nodded encouragingly.

Dolbin waited for Jakey to shilly-shally down to the counter. He stopped to tie a shoelace, straighten a card of pipe reamers. The color of his cheeks deepened; he stood motionless behind the register staring at his fingernails. He kept clearing his throat and saying "I." He then glanced pleadingly from Merce to Elvina, who flanked him. Their faces remained averted and impenetrable. He made a sharp protesting gesture with his wrist, as if to flick an insect away. When he finally spoke, his voice was barely a whisper and seemed to cause him great pain and embarrassment.

"I guess you want to go back to the old setup, huh?"

Dolbin nodded, half-mesmerized by the man's discomfiture. He said something very fast, to which Dolbin inclined his head, puzzled. Miserably, Jakey looked to Merce.

"Oh, for pity's sake," she said in a burst of exasperation. "He wants to know what you've done to deserve that right?"

Although he felt they could be had if it came down to polemics, instinct silenced him. It was necessary now to subordinate his claims to their opinion, however tactless and provincial. He shrugged his shoulders stupidly.

"He don't understand the basic tenets of Western redemptive theory," she said to Elvina.

"Well, he's abott to find ott," she replied and, like any other plumpish local matron, chuckled cheekily. Her face turned serious and she added, "We will grant you a full restoration of all former perquisities and favors. You will once again be counted among the rekler customers—but only upon the successful completion of certain requirements. Tell him, Chakey."

"Oh, okay," the man said peevishly. "First you must take all back issues, from your first Sunday in Vermont to the present. Counting today's, I believe that comes to forty-three weeks."

When Dolbin's eyes bugged in amazement, Elvina said, "We never throwed ott a one. We was chust testing you."

"How so?" he asked cautiously.

Merce: "Your capacity to accept loss graciously."

Jakey whispered something in her ear. She scowled and brushed him aside. "What fer dumb!" she said. "That was *not* it! We don't give a turnip's tooth how he comports himself in public!"

"I thought we wanted a quicker, more confident anger," said Elvina, "especially in the face of the kind of execration we dealt out. A little more verve—eloquence—in his own defense. We are talking here mainly about a failure of style."

"Eloquence?" Dolbin said thinly.

Merce scratched her head and looked perplexed. "And wasn't there something about social conscience? Did he even ask if we gave them to the poor, or rolled newspaper logs or used them to wrap garbage?"

"Well, anyhow," Jakie continued, "the second proviso stipulates that you read them—every last one—before you go home."

"You will be periodically quizzed on their contents," piped Elvina.

"And third—what's the third again, Viney?"

"A written pledge, duly bonded and notarized, that he will never again slap the *Times* importantly on the counter and treat the local rag as a Sunday supplement."

"Yes, yes, anything." He agreed to it all. Then he took the reading glasses from his shirt pocket.

The day he finished up, Jakey shook his hand and said, "Give the wife my best." So, of course, Dolbin knew that Mrs. Cee was gone. All these weeks without a word from him—he might hardly blame her but for his memory of her central role in all of this. How he had driven himself day and night to redeem the consequences of her waywardness; and every time he neared the end of the task, another Sunday had rolled around. Another Sunday, another edition. And now, half-blind, his stomach leadenly seeded with hard and gleeful fact, sickened by the ether smell of newsprint and all that remorseless perspicuity, he loaded the papers into his station wagon and headed home.

It had rained almost daily while he was gone, the neighbors said, their voices skillfully poised between censure and sympathy. The weeds came up to his collarbone. After a pounding summer downpour he pulled them all out. He soaked the newspapers in tubs of water; when he laid them out in the garden then, the moist summer breezes left them alone.

Mrs. Cee stopped by one day to look for the part of herself that was still attached, but said she couldn't stay long. She had a job as an inspector of No. 8 cabs at the local Mack plant. Before leaving she pointed out what was admittedly more of an idle observation than a relevancy, and certainly not a criticism in an age of everything being okay and all, that though the gardens boasted a certain cleanness of line and the overlay of leafmold provided a charmingly sylvan texture, she was hard put to find a single flower there.

And sometimes the neighbors appeared perplexed in passing, but in time came to bring their friends around to see the sprawling, impressive stretch of weedlessness. Some conjectured that it was probably an ascetic botanical style of Far Eastern or Indian provenance that he had picked up in his recent travels. Others commended him for the clarity of his personal statement.

For a while Dolbin made halfhearted, dutiful pilgrimages back to Bouch's so as not to offend people who had, after all, made every effort to be reasonable. Eventually he could not bring himself to go at all. The original condition was beyond discovery—locked as it was in the clear Lucite of his past, outstripped by its own legend; or worse, debased, distorted, disqualified by the price demanded for it and the price paid. And there were the difficulties with his eyes.

Dolbin knew that under the mulch, the weeds awaited only a suggestion of light, and under their shallow organic cover the words were beginning to swell, like dark seeds.

Janka Doodle

Let me tell you who lives in that house: small but solid three-bedroom ranch, nice corner lot, mature shrubs, sandbags heaped against the garage door, patio ringed by screens, blinds drawn; that crouching house battened against blows in a neighborhood of unlocked doors and lawns folding greenly together, of bicycles left out, and proud, announcing mailboxes. Well, Woodrow lives there, but he abides mainly with his God and attends to all proceedings with soft, sedated eyes. There are the thirtyish twins who come and go in delivery trucks, not paying much mind anymore to the vagaries of the household. And the crazy lady, not chained in the attic but loose, as a shoe is loose in a box. These sprigs of silver-dollar plant are for her. I picked them in my own woods.

We used to live in that house across the street. The white colonial with the foolish Doric columns on the skimpy portico. Having once been inspired by the exterior decor of Lutheran churches I painted the front door red, but the next people preferred a jaunty nautical blue, hired a professional landscaper and, all things considered, kept the place up much better than we did. I was very young when I tried to turn that house into a Lutheran church, a Village loft, a Slough of Disappointment—anything but a house—and Janka loved me like a daughter, even though she called me missus. She loved my small son, too. She brought us sour-cream potato salad and kielbasa and sometimes she borrowed things. I'd answer the door in the afternoon and find her standing there, a short, squarish woman toughened by duty and compulsiveness; her face broad, high-colored, handsome. She'd hold out a cup which I'd fill with vodka. And many times I'd see her pressing Woodrow's pants on the patio, pressing and singing, a split of champagne jiggling on the end of the ironing board.

She lured my husband and me at night with promises of cold cuts, Gibrovka, and music. Always about ten she would announce that Woodrow was a skate-cheap and a duddy-fuddy, then send him for his guitar. The mild, white-haired man would play his listless country songs—"Shenandoah," "Red River Valley," "On Top of Old Smoky"—always finish with Janka's native "Gur-alu," all of us singing a poor facsimile of the Polish words, knowing only that they were lovely and very sad. Once, long past midnight, when I suggested to my husband that we call it a night, Janka set her drink down hard and said with deadly calm: "Why do you hate me, Meesus Denney? You think I am Polish whore doorty?"

There were other auguries, had any of us been looking so many years ago. It was her habit to pop over in the mornings to "kidnap" my round, laughing son. She'd take him to her house all day and feed him sherbet and cubes of cinnamon toast and let him loose in the tiny jungle that was her "garden vegetable," an inhumanly prolific, bewitched place where he hid behind giant cabbages and sucked warm plum tomatoes and cucumbers no bigger than his thumb. Her own two boys were in their late teens; she missed their "not boniness," she said. And in those days, when I was nearly hermetically sealed in, I clawed my way out regularly (now that I am free, I never go anywhere). She often sat my child for me, indeed was indignant if I asked anybody else. One morning at first light she called to tell me I was a terrible mother and God would punish me. "You are selfish as dog," she said. At nine she phoned again to see if I would come over and sunbathe with her in the driveway, between the snowbanks, which I did. We lay there warm and wickedly bare against the more necessary nakedness of winter, sipping spiked lemonade and letting the straining February sun draw from our pallor just a suggestion of lurid pink.

And the business with Gwendolyn O'Hare who lived in the rough stucco bi-level two doors down from our old place, on the corner opposite Janka's. She was thirty, childless, and had befriended a boy we might have called, in other times, the village fool. In Willowood Estates he was Petie Siglo, trainable retarded. We got used to seeing Petie beat a path from his house to O'Hares', transistor pressed to one ear, the hand opposite hooked in like a garden claw. He might have been sixteen—it was hard to tell. He used to leave her house with old magazines, empty perfume bottles, carpet samples held possessively, pleasurably, against his cheek. When Janka first started making comments, we thought she was joking. And maybe at first she was, but the seminal thought fed some larger, darker reservoir that must have been like an edema against Janka's brain. The more she talked the larger the possibility of it grew and the higher the level of her agitation. She wept tears of sorrow and of anger. She began to fear obsessively for the chastity of her own sons; spotting them in Gwendolyn's front yard, Janka would stomp and scream them home again, as if they stood in mortal danger or on unholy ground. Within months the O'Hares were gone from the neighborhood. All of us felt very sorry for Gwendolyn, who remained objective and forgiving to the very end, but by then I would not or could not surrender the image I cherished of her soft gray eyes nudging Petie upstairs, her floating hands in the dim air, slowly, sweetly teasing back his fixity before the fullness of her blessing.

After Gwendolyn left, Lolly Hiester and I tacitly shouldered the emergent task of managing Janka. Lolly's was the diffident little Cape Cod between our house and the O'Hares'. She had a swaggering sixteen-year-old son for whom she peeled grapes and dispensed daily disaster warnings. She herself lived on the jittery edge of the worst of everything—the habit or the result (or the cause) of two bereavements in quick succession and a long stretch of dazed double widowhood. Unfit Mother and Chicken Little: We were the psychiatric council. We tried to calm Janka, steer her ever so adroitly away from the present into a past which was where we figured her rancor more properly directed. We questioned her about the war and worried her reluctance into an occasional blurted relevancy out of which I easily wove a full scenario:

She is painting her toenails when the Nazis come, because that's what I would have been doing at fifteen; or she is mending socks or lugging ashes in a tin pail, for surely she is different from me. . . . Whatever, the soldiers see the bright persistence of her polished coral toes and look away, embarrassed.

It is always November in this Polish border town, which I lay out to look like the lower end of Pelford, Pennsylvania: brick row houses with chalking white gables, wrought-iron fences, stubborn little yards. I add narrow cobbled streets and pushcarts, fish stalls, street musicians. The town is very still; the fiddlers hold their instruments behind their backs and suck in their breath. Even the pushcarts seem stalled, between worlds, awaiting a sidewalk sale or pots of plastic geraniums.

They put her in a holding cell that resembles the jerry-built jails they erect in all the American bicentennial towns. They arrange the people neatly in rows, like the apple slices on a good German *Kuchen*. Janka grips the bars (which are flimsy and brittle as old sticks—if she'd only look) and I notice her fingernails are the same preposterous pink, and somehow that gives me hope although I already know how the story always goes.

On her way home from the butcher shop where she stuffs sausages all day, Janka's mother is wiping her hands for the fortieth time on a clean muslin apron when she encounters this scene in the town square. She sees her round-faced Janka and another girl she never liked because of her chronic runny nose. At first she tries to tear away the spindly rails, which have by now hardened to a fateful, determined sturdiness. I keep thinking they should moan or cry or clutch each other through the bars, both so slow and silent, like old movies. The war, they are thinking, what can you do? I tell

125

myself it is different for people bound to the terms of a certain age. How graciously they go under the foot of the times, how quietly their worst fears assort to a calm history. Janka's mother gives up her babushka and walks home through mean thin air that's trying hard to produce a niggle of snow.

Janka is not a Jew, a fact that alters the train's passage across that empty, unimagined landscape. This lust is not for annihilation but for child labor. "Beeg bullets," she told me once. "In Germany I make beeg bullets." She remembers her mother and brother until they leach away in watery dreams. In her mattress she hides potatoes; they leave marks that fade to a tuberous yellow-brown on her hips. She wears a uniform like the green-skirted gym suit I once donned to play basketball with nuns at Pius X High. There is a large chestnut tree in the muddy camp yard. Janka and her new friends ping chestnuts off the tin roof of their barracks and bowl them under marching soldiers' feet. The tree is cut down and splinters are sealed in little cellophane packets which Janka is forced to peddle up and down the streets of Mannheim. Relics of the True Family Tree. For the war effort.

Long after Janka distinctly allowed how she was raised in the tenant house of a millionaire's country estate, I continued to insist upon that cold November town and the stilled pushcarts. And Lolly and I kept pressing her, driving for catharsis. *What else did the bastards do?* Then whatever she had said or hinted, she would dismiss with a sweep of her arm, saying, "Nazis always very good to me. Nobody ever touch me with doorty Joorman stick."

Woodrow is the tall young American soldier who

gathers her in after the war.. They go home to his mother, who waits on some shaded southern porch, waits with camomile tea and not a hint that this is not the daughter-in-law she dreamed. This scruffy, tubercular, uninterpreted girl. Okay, okay, I invent and I finagle— how do I know what kind of tea? But is it not reasonable that Woodrow's temperate sort of decency accrued to him from somewhere, from soft Maryland summers and slow-lapping streams, from a mother who waited slack and tender-eyed on clean porches?

In the midst of our ministrations to Janka it was Lolly who had the nervous breakdown. Her son Parker had graduated from high school and wanted to cross the street alone. Next it was cars and beer and before she could stop him, he'd entered the police academy. Janka brought her *halupkis,* sour cherries steeped in grain alcohol, and shortly after that *we* moved away.

I am not good at keeping in touch, not at first. My initial need is to sever all those frazzled ties, cleanly and for good—my only and most contemptible neatness. Then months, sometimes years, later I find myself inexplicably wrenched off course and speeding to the old places, ringing the doorbells of people who squint through peepholes, guessing me. In time then, in much the same way, I went back to Willowood, and then I couldn't stay away. I returned again and again, sniffing, expectant, starved for myself or something better. Was this a sign of age?

The spindly subdivision locust trees grew and began to provide modest shade, an aura of establishment. My old front door, as I said, went from red to blue. Then black. Janka's garden got bigger and then it got smaller.

I don't know when I first noticed the air had begun to thicken and draw and settle to a sullen ineluctability.

It seemed everything stayed fairly level for several years after we left. Then, as Janka sat stalled in a thru-way traffic jam, a Volkswagen bus rear-ended her—a nudge, a tap; no more. She was not hurt but began to believe exclusively in the Next Time and knew it had been no accident.

Her brother came from Poland and refused to go back. Brother and sister spent hours staring into the crude, unbreakable mirrors of their parallel histories. They discovered how each had been subdued—she in Germany, he in Poland—with threats to the other's person. They held each other responsible for the years of internment and ruined youth; each demanded full credit for the other's survival. One evening I sat at Janka's table and watched her and Casimir slug down shots of tinted vodka and curse each other in Polish. Woodrow played "Greensleeves" on the taut strings of his endless patience. He kept saying, "Janka, this man is your brother." And then, in his courtly way, he would offer me another Chablis.

The next time I came Janka impounded my handbag and examined the contents. She handed it back with the practiced dourness of a customs agent. The neighborhood had changed, she said. She took me to the window and pointed to Gwendolyn's old house. "They watch me day and night," she said. "I am scared like dog." Her small tartar eyes narrowed shrewdly, appraising my own sidelong glance. She went on: "Children come by on bicycles, call out, 'Dirty Janka, red-face

Janka!' I am shake like dog all time," she says, holding out her hands.

She pointed to the blue door. "Meesus, they stand in yard bold as dogs, point weapons that make no noise and is made to look like hose garden." I offered her sympathy, wisdom, maturity beyond my years, another chance to damn the Nazi barbarians. She brushed me away: *"They* were nice," she said. She turned off the air-conditioner, covered the vents so we would not be overheard. Somewhere between our two realities we met and held hands for a while, and then it was *my* ground that began to crumble. I lowered my voice and watched the window and could no longer be so easily seduced by the assurances of her polished, sunstruck Formica.

When I went to Lolly's she yanked me inside. "Hurry," she said. "Come in before Janka sees you. She'll think we're talking about her."

"We are."

"She'll think we're hatching plots."

"She doesn't trust *you* anymore?"

Lolly wobbled her hand, yes and no. "Mostly it's Parker. He's a security guard at the Steel. Because of his eyes, you know—I mean that's why he couldn't make the force, thank God. It's the uniform. When she sees him dressed she always says she loves him the same as when he was a child, but why did he have to go and get involved with *Them* and do those terrible things."

I believe we each had a mental image of the galumphing, blustery harmlessness of her Parker. She drew deeply on her cigarette and smiled the smoke through her teeth. She described a new mycin she'd been on for

129

her asthma. Using textbook medicalese always seemed to soothe her nerves. Then she told me how Janka had grabbed the sample aerosol deodorant out of the salesman's hand and chased him down the walk, spraying the thing full blast, like some kind of fiendish, sidewinding human crop-duster.

I said, "Poor Janka," and immediately a volley of laughter ripped out of my chest. Then Lolly got started. We put our heads on the counter and choked our guilty giggles into the cold tiles. Even though we took turns trying to say, It's not funny, It's not funny, it was surely one of the funniest things we'd ever heard.

After the handbag incident Janka never suspected me of anything again. Even that once, I believe, was merely a gesture, a stroke of habit, a wily preparation, perhaps, for the horror stories she was dying to tell me. (She was never without a finely honed sense of the baroque.) I was gone from the neighborhood; no part of my house was trained menacingly against her pathetic fortifications; no windows watching, no drain spout twisted queerly. No ominous hardware on *my* rooftop yawing after the night sounds of her household. I believe, too, she remembered my helplessness in the white colonial. Could I, who left my handbag in supermarket parking lots, whose child got out at four in the morning to ring doorbells and beg bananas, could I aspire to these marvelous conspiracies? Surely she recalled dressing me the morning I could not get out of bed, leading me to the table, holding the cup while I sipped my tea. Is this the style of a high-powered hit woman? And all those times she rescued me from the clutter of a normal afternoon; how, scolding, she helped my boy pick up his puzzles and Lincoln Logs, tossed the cushions back on the chairs and shook my springs loose, set me into squeaky motion again. No, even at its largest and fullest, her dementia could not have allowed for so preposterous a complicity.

She bought a bright-yellow canary. We called it Litmus behind her back, for its purpose was to test the air. The idea came out of the coal mines; if the bird survived the poison gases, so perhaps might she. In addition she acquired a large gray dog with eyes the color of autumn skies. One day the blue-eyed dog ate the yellow canary, and nothing was determined about the pervasiveness of evil.

All of our boys died their many deaths quietly. The toddlers are gone, the baseball players, the practicing pubescents. My son left his teenage skin on the porch one day and went to live in the wilderness. So sometimes I went back to the old neighborhood because I was hungry for him, for the haunts of his "not boniness." I began to wish I had stayed home more when he was three. And Janka's twins, long grown up, never left at all. They turned out to be handsome young men, but not identical: one tall and fair-haired like Woodrow, the other small, compact, ruddy like his mother. In time they learned not to be embarrassed when their mother stood in the yard sicking the devil on their friends or hurling tiny hard apples and Polish curses at passing bicycles and cars. She cooked for them and cleaned their rooms, and there were periods when she was actually ashamed of her behavior. On her good days the boys liked to pinch her cheeks and call her Janka Doodle.

They went into identical but separate businesses. We are independents, they'd say happily. Each serviced a different territory for the same company, drove identical vans that said *PULSINGER'S BAKERY* in squeezed green-icing letters. Woodrow added a second section of paved driveway, parallel to the first, so the vehicles could enjoy equal off-street parking and so the neighbors—who'd never dare—would not complain.

Every Wednesday the boys went back to their markets to restock shelves and pick up the week's "stales." All this they brought home to Janka, trays full of rolls and breads and pastries, just past their date. She could have her very own bread route, they teased. They made her their stales manager and gave her a paper baker's hat that said PULSINGER'S. Occasionally she'd call and tell me to come and get some freebies. "I am busy as dog dese days," she'd say importantly. "I can't deliver so far— this week I have good crumb cake and potato roll." I see her so clearly:

Janka has a very old wagon with removable wooden sides and wonderful double rear wheels which she piles high with the boys' stales. Up and down the streets of the neighborhood she goes, knocking on doors, calling yoo-hoo into open kitchen windows. Although she doesn't really wear the silly paper hat, she does keep it in the wagon, should her authenticity come into question. To the same people she has already this week accused of wire-tapping, attempted arson, conspiracy, germ warfare, she offers butter-baked, almost fresh amends, all they can stuff in their freezers. Some accept her bags with careful, self-conscious gratitude. The lady who lives in my old house now comes out, grabs the bread, and slams the flat black door so I can't see that the inside of that place no longer exists.

So here I stand next to my husband in Janka's doorway, with my armload of lustrous silver dollars. I plucked the pods carefully so none would tear. Each single perfect disc shimmers like pearly watered silk. I wanted to give her something, for all the stales, for no reason really.

"Tanks," she says and looks at me with swollen purple eyes; her face appears slightly off center. "That doortie boordie Casimir broke. my nose."

"Be fair, Janka," says Woodrow soberly. "Tell the Denneys what *you* did first."

Her gaze drops coyly; she affects a momentary remorse before announcing with sudden, ill-concealed glee. "Dese teet bite him right here." She points to her own shoulder. Woodrow nods a rueful confirmation.

Seeing my husband's puzzling gaze on the steep bunker of sandbags, she says, "They geev me no choice, Meester Denney." Then, "You come in. We have party, like old days."

Woodrow says, do, do stay. We exchange glances. Well, *Maybe, for a little while.*

Janka phones Lolly, who comes right over; the Slovaks, who live in Gwendolyn's old house—Communist swine only yesterday—who do not.

How pleasant then; it seems we have never been away, Janka slicing ham and arranging pickle slices; Janka complaining of frayed rugs and Woodrow's parsimoniousness; Woodrow sitting quiet and happy to see us. The boys get back from the beach. They have always been charming, hospitable. They sit on the same stools at the kitchen counter and smile at us as Janka brings them frosty drinks in the same tall glasses. They have wonderful white teeth against their summer tans and fine hard bodies that stir me pleasantly until I remember Gwendolyn, and even then.

Lolly is as silly after one drink as ever. She and Janka hug each other a lot and say things like, "We have our moments but. . ." Occasionally Janka slips a sly jab at "big bullyboy storm trooper," meaning Parker, but Lolly is having fun, her asthma is fine, and she lets everything go by.

The boys loosen up, start to trade hearty stories about the evangelists that come around: Francine, the Witness: Candy, the Born Again; Jim, the Mormon. How do they get wind of such pickings? I wonder. How do potato beetles find out you've planted potatoes? They say that sometimes it happens all of them arrive at the same time, with their tracts and pamphlets and wholegrain faces. I picture Janka playing hostess to this gospel gala; surely she'd serve lemonade and poppy-seed roll and whip their rival ardors into a fine stiff froth, all the while playing dumb and undecided, to keep them all coming back.

Woodrow chides the boys mildly. "They're well-meaning people. We can always use a little more God in this house."

"They tell me I am good person except I drink like dog," Janka says sullenly.

"Like a fish," from one of the boys.

When she starts in about the secrets and the spies, nobody listens but me—and Woodrow in his oblique, abstracted way. The boys and my husband talk jogging shoes and sailboats. Lolly slumps in her chair smiling foolishly. Janka is quick to sense the softness of my edges, that I can be had. She knows I am beginning to recognize the saboteurs in the neighborhood, the hard cases, the false fronts, the folks who only pretend to be hooking up central vacuum systems and gas grills. Woodrow knows it too. He watches uneasily lest I up and confirm everything, go out and help stack sandbags against the garage. "I am dopy as fish," she says, testing the air. "Dees stuff they put take long time to kill you." I feel myself getting groggy and dart my tongue around suspiciously. I detect a faint, sweetish undertaste but hasten to say, "Nonsense!" offering Woodrow a collusive glance. But it is he I'm doing the number on. How can they *not* believe her?

Speaking of her psychiatrist then, she works herself into a rage that brings tears to her eyes. "How can one little dummy man save me from all this terrible thing?" she asks.

"Tell her what you did to undermine Dr. Pearl's best efforts, Janka." This from Woodrow. She drops her chin.

"Jaaaaanka!"

"I plop my pills in hees coffee, see how he like, dees poison he give me. He call may-dee-ceen but I know how it make me sick as fish, make me feel two place one time. Beside, he call me filty Polish field whore," she adds quickly, almost coyly.

"Sick as a *dog*, Janka," Woodrow says softly.

Then she shows me the spot where her wondrous garden used to be—all grass now except for a single tomato plant and a clump of Chinese parsley. Her patio expands in concentric circles of self-defense; drawn

135

bamboo shades to a ring of untrimmed, overgrown, tufting junipers—ghostly in the early dark—to a double border of folding louvered screens. "Remember, Meesus," she says, "how we used to lay under God's wonderful beeg sun, days when you and me and dees country still free."

For the first time I see how white she is—a prison pallor—that she is grown fat and old and that I, reflected in the sliding glass door, am nearly as fat and old as she was then. Panicked, I look around for somebody to blame, some whispering cabal—but it is only Woodrow come to reel his wife back in. "Janka," he says, taking her arm, "Come, it's time to sing."

Woodrow's hand has no force, no future, I notice. It drops down like a plumb bob over the face of his guitar, again and again, a hand induced by the weight of faith and gravity to support a habit of simple chords. We all join together for several verses of "Guralu," even the bronzed, handsome boys, reluctantly. Lolly's arm is around Janka's shoulder; Janka laughs because we don't get the Polish words quite right. We're probably singing something blasphemous or dirty.

Days go by before word reaches me. Even then the information is given respectfully, with dry-mouthed restraint; a few tough-knuckled facts meant to betoken a proper spareness, a mature affection for the objective truth. But my version, I believe, is no less decorous, nor less true:

Lolly has gone up to take an afternoon nap when she hears the car. She looks out the bedroom window and sees Parker backing into the driveway. The air is syrupy thick with sunlight and summer dust—and various fragrances, she imagines, how sweet and winy; she is so glad to see him. He has been missed in the months since he took his downtown apartment. She watches him emerge in his crisp gray uniform (at thirty, there is the beginning of dignity, the start of a red, rather dashing moustache). He walks to the back of his car and raises the lid of the trunk. He is rearranging something or looking for something. By now she accepts, understands the dull bluish glint of his revolver; it is no more, no less than a button, a zipper, a diacritical mark over the word hip.

The moment she sees Janka she cries out, pounds on the window, but Parker has left the motor running and the muffler is bad or he refuses to hear out of a lifetime of not listening. She wants to run downstairs but is held by the absurd but essential belief that her eye on him is some kind of amulet against harm. Lolly stares across to the sudden false green, the unremembered dreamy terrain of Janka's yard and sees whole armies. But it is only Janka, now hurdling the cotoneaster, short legs pumping, holding to a straight course, across the road now, charging with the compressed passion of a discus thrower. In her upraised hand, held splendidly—like a ceremonial torch—is a length of galvanized pipe. When she reaches the driveway she glances up at Lolly; their eyes fill a single instant with centuries. Everything is begged and everything forgiven. Then Janka revs the pipe, skirling the air, and almost as a carelessness, catches the bent Parker across the back of the head.

Lolly flies down the stairs and out through the garage. She leaps at Janka and wrestles her to the ground. The two women struggle and curse and whimper, flail at each other harmlessly, like marionettes. They have both waited too long for this to be made suddenly wild. Parker, who has pitched forward at the moment of impact, lies slightly creased at the waist, with his head deep in the trunk, as if he had crawled in to make a myopic search of the interior grit. The day just hangs there limp and sallow and stupid; August is an impossibly lumpish month to be pressing down on a man from such a height . . . but in time I always bring Parker around, gently, as if he were my very own. Slowly, his body teeters back the other way, his feet find their bottoms, and he sets himself carefully aright. He stands watching the listless combat on the macadam, uncomprehending as a sleep-walker. Here is where my camera has to stop; an eye closes over a gash of time. All of us saying filthy fucking Hitler, Nazi bastards, vile pigs: moral surgeons, tying off blame, as if it all began *there* . . . and ended here, on this day, in this neighborhood, in this driveway; as if evil might be dammed up between places and people and calendar years, held back until we, the watchers, are far enough away. Or have ourselves occasion for it.

Then I set my camera in motion again, not the next day perhaps, but in a month or two. Janka Doodle, busy as a fish, loading up her wagon. The boys handing her sticky buns and whole-wheat muffins. She puts on a light sweater because it is autumn. The sharp October skies, the crystal air cut her like glass. She goes to my old house first and no matter how hard I try now, I can't get the red off that door. When nobody answers, she leaves her baked goods on the porch, a loaf of cinnamon raisin, molasses cakes, and sticky buns because she knows I could never do anything with yeast. At Lolly's she waits a long time for the door to open. When it does, Lolly is still in her brushed-nylon nightgown, rubbing her eyes even deeper into the purplish hollows. At Janka's side, the silver-gray dog, motionless; his head holds flashes of limitless, lustrous, empty sky and dim memories of easy yellow feathers. The two women stare at each other for a long while before Janka gathers up her loaves and, cradling them, lays them timidly across Lolly's thin branching arms.

A Wrestler's Tale

Nobody'd ever call him a takedown specialist, but he gets the first two points this time. A go-for-it ankle pick, clean and rhythmic. One. Two. Ka-boom. His kid smells like the inside of a soup can—or something—and maybe that's how he gets reversed. Too high on the cradle while he ponders the essences rising off the Valley High fish. *Concentrate, dumdum.*

Too late. That quickly he's flailing like a hooked trout, cradled himself. Legs pedaling air. No damn leverage. Valley fans thundering for blood. *Pin. Pin.* No way is he getting decked. He knows that from the start. Kid isn't in on him that tight. Not enough time on the clock. The hungry roar splits and out of it grows the stem of his mother's voice. High, clear, panicked, as if her fear is that he is about to die. *Bobbeeeee. Bobbeeeeee.* And then *Bobbe.* . . . An amputation and a slack gray bellying-out of time into which his name drops and is swallowed like a weapon discarded in shame and horror.

His memory grew fat with remembering, plumped up with that sweet, stale air and her voice. Her voice, his name. Her voice, his name. Yet could he actually have heard her at the time? During a match nothing ever seemed to penetrate his will and need to win. The area of the mat measured out a walled space within which he functioned blind and deaf to the cross fire coming from the stands: *shoot, shoot, stand up, cross face, hit it.* If the cheerleaders got up and delivered their grunt sounds and nonsense rhymes for his sake, then that exercise was lost on him as well. *Bobbeeeee, Bobbeeeeee, Bobbe.* . . . Had it registered subliminally, then curled up inside and waited out a short gestation before becoming all there was?

More likely it was the telling and retelling that had been the fruitful seeding of his memory. How many times had he been made to listen? That night, then at the funeral home, where she had looked so young, younger than himself, younger than his girl, Heidi Ann, younger than she had ever been in her whole life. He, ashamed to look at her in that high-necked pink thing like a baby's dress, ashamed as if he had walked in on her at a bad time, in the bathtub or on the john. Everybody moving in so close, talking out of their special-occasion selves, their faces gone boneless, their voices converging on that one strangled moment when she had half-stood in the bleachers, steadied her hand on his dad's shoulder, and called to him, and called again, and suddenly clutched her head, most likely at the precise moment when his name had exploded with a soundless soft pop in her brain.

He began to shy from the sound of that unremarkable set of syllables—Baw-bee—though, in the main, it came to him from bland and harmless places: the lips of his teachers, the core of Heidi Ann's giggles, the locker room. Sometimes he winced as though struck. And there were those times when his teeth were set on edge and his temples pulsed violently. That was when the man who was his father spoke—and it mattered not the context or tone—his name. Then he was filled with a befouled blackness, a sense of irradicable taint. He saw complicity at any point where they touched, and in their combined maleness a blunt instrument linked somehow to that orderly death and his own damnation. "Call me that again," he said to his father at last, "and I'll kill you."

"Poof! A ruptured aneurysm of an intracranial artery. That's all," Mr. Winger said. *That's all* came out small and squeaky and peevish. He was just a psychological counselor, not a psychiatrist, they'd assured him: "Just call him plain old Mister." Plain old Mr. Winger went on impatiently: "A congenital timebomb. If not that night, the next day, next week. Poof."

Yes, he understood. Fact was fact. (Poof!) But he would still prefer the first name that was, after all, legal and proper and rightly his. His birth certificate said George Robert Parsley. He would take the George now, thank you.

When the hour was up, Mr. Winger seemed thankful. "Same time next week, Bobby?"

With their curious blend—peculiar it seems to fifteen-year-olds—of defenselessness and defiance, plus a suggestion of polite disdain, his eyes fought back.

"Uh, George," Mr. Winger mealymouthed, offering miserly amends.

Reluctantly his sister, who was a year older, obliged. Bridget enunciated a Bostonese *Jaw-gee,* as if making it silly enough absolved her own sense of silliness. R. Waldo Parsley avoided, when he could, calling his son anything at all. Back against the wall, though, he said *George*, and as the weeks passed he hesitated less and less before the name slipped into his life stealthily as a changeling child. Such compliance advanced his cause but little. The boy still accused him silently, beat him down with his relentless remembering. I saw you, he said with unlit eyes, I saw you push her and she went down on one knee and looked afraid. I heard you on the phone; you couldn't get enough of someone named Barb. You left her alone too much. You left the dirty jobs to her, the dog crap, the broken glass. Spilled your Hershey syrup on the rug and ran. *I dare you to cry, you bastard.*

In school the word got around and some of his teachers eventually succumbed to his hangdog obstreperousness, mostly women. Then Mr. Legus, a sensitive-type Lit teacher, began self-consciously to say *George*. Some of the kids, too, more girls of course than boys.

"Give this to George," someone might say, and when it was handed to George Leiby: "No, no, I mean Bobby." *Oh, that George.*

After the funeral his first deliberate act was to quit the wrestling team. How was he to sit again on that same bench? He'd thought somebody fainted. He was impatient to get on with the match. He was down 5–2. At first, as they carried her past the bench, he hadn't recognized her. Her lips were the color of street ice aging in shadow. But that was *his* rust turtleneck she was wearing, and on her feet the "sheepdog" boots, those awful furry things she wore to the slopes. Her face was dead. No face could be sucked so pale and yet live. His dad carrying her tooled handbag and his camera, nose pecking at the air, rushing right on by.

Only Mrs. Imbody stopped. She squeezed his shoulders for a second, and meaning to give instant, hurried solace, said, "She had your name on her lips, dear." Then, as he stood gawking, they went by, the entire entourage, it was like a river that was there and gone, and the river was white and frozen and too cold to touch.

The very second thing he did was re-join the team. What else was there after school but to go home with Bridget and her stiff upper lip and help make sunflower-seed patties or tofu-and-peanut soup for supper (when had Bridget's dietary theories become their law?), and wait for the old man to come home soft and sappy and pitiable (hadn't *she* always ended up feeling sorry for him?) in the wake of an extended cocktail hour? Nobody wanted his "two wunnaful kids a mine" talk then, his oozy, uncharacteristic affection slopping over into shop gibberish, the professional laments of a tipsy trial lawyer on a losing streak. "My client is always innocent," he was fond of saying, trying his damnedest to sound wry, "until I prove him guilty."

At least he had the good sense not to try talking about *her*. The man would go to bed early then, forgoing the tofu, and sometimes as George-Bobby passed his open door, he heard him cry. *Crocodile tears!* Remember how you broke her best antique doll in one of your conniption fits! Remember good old Barb! But he had memories of his own: a ten-spot lifted from a purse, a raised fist, his voice wearing her down to pain for the sake of a new tape deck, a go-cart, a trip to the shore; the way she kept loving him, giving in to it as if she could not

manage to do otherwise, as if one of them were right-
fully born to it.

His father's tears would seem to invite him, the big
unmade bed like a warm and holy place. Just as it appeared nothing could hold him back a second longer,
he was walking swiftly to his own room, where the distance from the ceiling to the bed, he knew, measured
roughly the depth of a standard grave.

He asked his father to please not bother coming to
his matches. He probably wouldn't win anyway, he said.
This he did knowing the extent of the man's pleasure
in his son's contending, how early he came home on
meet nights, how happily he set about gathering film
and the new sound camera that was, to the boy, only
an emblem of the man's excessiveness. In this, also, R.
Waldo Parsley complied.

All the more time for your girlfriend, Waldo.

And he was wrong about not winning. Indeed, it was
impossible to lose. His strivings seemed to spring from
a fresh source, a core of pure effort, washed clean of
fear and face, of theatrics, of all urge to glory, of him
actually. He wrestled entirely in his wrestler's body, and
it knew the way, always. Because nothing much mattered to his larger life, it was powerless to choke off the
surge of its lesser turnings. He was free. He knew the
precise moment to hit a pancake, to go in for the single
leg. Without a second's pause he sensed the readiness
of his kid to be arm-barred or cradled. To the crowd's
intrusion he was more immune than ever. But Bridget
told him it was *very* confusing. They were yelling for
George and Bobby and his opponent. "Like there were
three guys out on the mat," she said.

*   *   *

Mr. Winger narrowed his eyes. "You feel double-crossed somehow?" Then, settling almost gleefully on the apter term: "Ripped off?"

"No, sir, I feel—most of the time—like a jerk."

"Small wonder, fella, you without a name."

"I have a name," said he.

Heidi Ann called him George when she remembered. Heidi Ann, the cheerleader. Builder of pyramids, counting and chanting and spelling out her counsel. Nice, but for the legs. Local stock quality, Pennsylvania Dutch piano legs. She tried to talk some sense into him. *Sticks and Stones* . . . but she called him George anyway and baked molasses cakes and bought him a $6.98 Crosby, Stills and Nash "to take his mind off things." But she pried his fingers from her thigh and layered wooly thicknesses between him and her breast.

"Come on, Hide," he pleaded repeatedly, "you could help if you wanted."

"No, George, I can't." She was firm. And when he pressed, she whined, "Stop it, Bobby. You're being unfair."

From the bench he watched his team's lightweights take their punishment. *Lousy damn puss outfit!* He lost interest, found himself intent upon the league ref instead. A slight black man, slim and supple as a stick of licorice. More grace in his little finger . . . each act of judgment a balletic triumph. Watch him circle the combatants, panther-like, sleek as silk. Now crouched with one leg extended, balanced on the edges of his shoes, now poised back on his heels, now leaping, knife-limbed from one side of the locked bodies to the other, dropping weightlessly down to judge the back points. Face full of wit, mock-wonderment, laughing at the crowd making such a case of a schoolboy romp. Look at me, he seemed to say. I am a moth among the bullfrogs. I am lighter than light.

George-Bobby dreamed that night a dancer's dream. No heaven, no earth, but a shimmering blue in-betweenness that was all his, a fullness of space granting him leave to soar. He was aware of not wanting to abuse this privilege, and the essence of the dream became a kind of deference to undefined limits, a certainty of ceiling. A slow unwinding desire for it. Still, every line his body assumed, every angle, every suspended vault upward, was pure and perfect and sure. Upon waking, he was shocked to remember that he was not a dancer but a second-rate wrestler having a good year.

He slept again and dreamed again, this time of *her.* Sitting up in that baby-pink nylon nightgown, horribly, mechanically animated, like the masterwork of some fiendishly inventive undertaker. The mouth was in motion seconds before any sound came out; her arms gestured woodenly. The voice was slow, measured, scratchily metallic as though it were being raked across miles of rusted roofing tin. It said, "Look at pretty Joanie. Kiss me, kiss me, kiss me."

He awoke too terrified to cry out, angry that *she* should haunt him so, then full of blame and shame for having conjured her up so obscenely. He began to whimper loudly enough to wake somebody, but no comfort came to him out of the steep night silences.

He drifted away from Heidi Ann. Melody Beiber lived with her mother and boyfriend in a two-bedroom trailer. Melody did not find the boyfriend loathsome, merely leprous. Saturdays she cleaned the horse stalls at Leather Corner Post Farm in exchange for riding privileges. When George-Bobby came by on his bike, she offered him a ride, too, and on later occasions he climbed with her to the loft. *George* came easy to her, not having known *Bobby* at all. She was generous, tractable as Tess, the ancient broodmare. He became a small, burrowing, furry thing; he emerged always more alone than he had ever been. They clung and separated and came clumsily together again. He was afraid to let go, afraid of the cold wedging in between. She hung on with tendrils like rusted wire. Their bodies made a damp, malodorous heap, it seemed to him, as limp and shapeless as the pile of sopping weight-sucking sweats dumped out of his gym bag each night.

"I don't enjoy wasting your dad's money. Do you, George?"

"I don't know. Do I?" Mr. Winger seemed on the verge of tears, florid with failure, but the boy, though remorseful, was powerless to rescue him.

Everybody said how well Bridget had adjusted. Dug right in at home, baked whole wheat bread and kept the place cleaner than her mother ever had and all the time maintaining B's at school. They said it more to emphasize the boy's intransigence. While he worked out at Nautilus, his mind nibbled at small irrelevancies. He envisioned his sister's body knobbed like a hobnail vase.

148

Control buttons for every occasion. Adjusting. And the thought of her textured flesh made his skin crawl over screaming muscles.

Actually he liked his sister. Proud and independent and tough. She never pushed him; gave him his moods, his maladjustments. Only she understood, or pretended to, about that vision of his name ripping through *her* last moment on earth. His name awash in blood and brains. His name a high red killer.

Sometimes she came to his room and they smoked a joint, and talk of her was an easy exercise: how she skied her heart out for years and never got beyond advanced-intermediate, her mind-buckling fear of ice; the perpetual astonishment with which she viewed them, her children, that they should be at all and be so fine; how alike were mother and son, given to the mystical and more than a little absentminded, forever locking themselves out and leaving their most treasured earthly goods in school yards and parking lots and public restrooms. But as they traded anecdotes, Bridget might slip in a line such as "She could dish it out, too, you know—with the best of them," intending sly exoneration of their father. Mostly, though, they were careful to exclude mention of the man, so sometimes the stories came out distorted, off-center as the first clay bowls Bridget threw on the potter's wheel.

He was full of love for his sister. She was beautiful and they would never be parted. Together, while the acrid haze deepened, they traveled the Mind of the Universe, glimpsed the Meaning of Life. On these nights he slept deeper than his pain.

It was Saturday. February now. Winter hardened into

a state of mind. The sameness of those Saturday afternoons: listless flurries over a stiff landscape, grayness tumbling, his father napping and reading and watching basketball by turns, Bridget mixing up a batch of granola. Pre-meet butterflies in his stomach, and also hunger pangs. A pound and a half over the night before. He dared not munch out, not even a carrot stick. The constant deprivation gave him a feeling of cleanness of line and a sense of moving closer to his own center. Soupbone, *she* had called him.

But the texture of those afternoons seemed to shrivel him; poky hours, predictable as the prints left by a three-legged dog. Bridget, who generally tried to mobilize them constructively on weekends, wanted to move a brass bed from the garage to her room. Their father pointed to an old repaired hernia, his status as a wage earner, the weather. But the bed was a heavy, unwieldy affair, a task for at least three.

"Come on, man, the weekend goof-off is over. This isn't Mom, it's bad-ass Bridget. Damn it, give us a hand."

"He makes me sick," the boy muttered to his sister. Their father flung *National Geographic* to the carpet, threw up his hands in a parody of a gesture that was unfortunately in earnest.

"Jerk!" from the boy, and the two fair-haired young people started down to the garage.

"Don't start anything," Bridget warned, "Or he'll quit on us."

It was a minor undertaking enlarged by the customary intimations of major personal hardship; Saturday surliness, breach of an unwelcome peace, a force that got things done. The last piece to be portaged was the heavy iron spring platform.

"It's this thing's the kicker," Bridget said, straining against her corner.

"At least hold up your crummy little end, Dad," George-Bobby said, accepting his sister's sharp glance. He'd taken on a whole side by himself. Wrestling muscles versus fortyish flab teamed with soft girl-flesh.

It was an open but narrow stairway. No room to edge around the side and steady the thing. So it tipped and dipped and tilted dangerously over the railing. Somebody had to be to blame.

"Jesus crackers, people," puffed Bridget.

"He doesn't give a shit."

Hearing this, the man let go. His children were momentarily thrown off-balance before he retook and steadied his grip.

"Puss!" from his son.

"Gees-um!" from his daughter.

He replied to them both. "Wiseasses! Coupla wiseasses!"

At the top of the stairs was a tight corner. Two and a half feet of carpet, a covered radiator, a window. The boy ordered the platform lifted, eased flat over the railing, turned on end and brought back around the stairway opening straight into Bridget's room.

"Bunch of Mickey Mouse," his father said. Better to take it straight up to the top, stand it on end, tip it slightly and "right in, slick as a whistle."

"Slick as a whistle, shit!"

"Lay off, asshole. This thing's slicing my hand off!"

151

"Okay, let the infant have his way. Baby Waldo!"

A chunk of plaster was gouged from the wall, leaving a dent shaped like a slice of liver. They nicked the walnut banister and chipped pumpkin paint from the molding around Bridget's doorway. In a paroxysm of mutual effort they raised up the platform. Shards of caramel-colored leaded glass rained down on their heads.

"I told ya. Now we broke her best Tiffany lamp."

"Tiffany-style," corrected Bridget.

But with the hall fixture gone the thing was easily maneuvered the few remaining feet. They dropped it heavily in the center of Bridget's room.

Bridget began to circle, taking long strides. She dropped down on her knees, sifting and picking among the brass and iron hardware, long yellow hair atumble. The boy suddenly remembered Little Granny. Years ago already, *she* had called Bridget that. Little Granny, because the child presided so wisely, stood sad-eyed guard over general family incompetence, and had all their numbers from the start. When she looked up, George-Bobby took a quick step back. Her eyes were brown bullets, her mouth set hard. Little Granny was nothing short of emergent matriarch, executrix of the New Order. She could eat us alive, she could, it occurred to him.

"This part snaps into this." She motioned and pointed. "One of you on this end. George, get down here." How easily she said his name.

Their obedience was immediate, almost eager. "You'll have to hold that steady till Dad gets that doojigger in."

From his station behind the brass head section, he looked down at the circle of skin marking the top of his dad's bent head. Hog-belly pink. Only part the man exposed to the world. Doubly vulnerable then. Strike him now, hairless, defenseless creature.

He aimed the words like drops of spittle. "You didn't care about Mom's good lamp, did you?"

A pause, a laborer's grunt. "No, the light meant nothing to me." The metal tenon kept slipping out of the slot.

"And you didn't give a rat's ass about her"; the words biting down on something hard enough to hurt the boy's teeth.

Throwing his shoulder into the effort, the man said, "Damn, maybe this piece belongs on the other side."

"Why don't you change the subject or something?"

"Let him alone." Bridget's face, pale as cream.

"Oh, sure! Protect the big baby!" His mouth clogged with something like small, hard seeds. Very slowly he cracked their bitter hulls. He said, "Do you remember what your wife looked like, W-Waldo?" He tried to suck back a sob.

He became aware that his father hadn't moved a muscle in many minutes. Time swelled the space between them, pressed his anger flat, his tears dry. *Bridget, don't go yet.*

Then as he looked down, the bald spot slid slowly back, and beneath him instead, his father in full face: A reply? An admission? Whose eyes were those, burning cold in their tearlessness? Never had he seen the man so close, so rawly. Or was it just his dad, unveiling despair as if it were new art? A Baby Waldo trick. Never had he hated him so much—or loved him more. Never had he felt such contempt, and pity. He wanted to move closer; he wanted to run far from the field of that indeterminate gaze.

Then his father said, "Dumb shit! Dumb shit!" and bent again to his task.

Later, after the bed was assembled, Bridget made it up with the quilt she'd sewn herself and the matching shams. He gave it a light polish with Brasso. It looked crisp and orderly and serene. Bridget set her mother's Floradora doll rakishly against the pillows. The doll wore a drop-waist dress of beige lace and a straw hat festooned with tiny Michaelmas daisies. One foot pointed painfully northeast.

The boy went downstairs then. In the room where his father sat sulking and smoking and watching barrel jumpers on *Wide World of Sports,* he fiddled for a while with his beebee maze, flipped through magazines. He began to rub at a water ring on the end table. "Match is at home tonight," he told his father in low tones.

He is doing a number on his kid; 19–0 at the start of the third period. Tonight he is a magician with a bottomless bag of tricks. He's hit a Japanese whizzer, a standing Gramby, a couple of Jacobs, a Peterson. He can do anything on this kid. The fans are enraptured, calling out and coaxing further astonishments.

He senses the nose of his father's camera, and he performs smoothly as a porpoise for the sake of that distant whir signaling the man's reconstituted pride. How odd that he should hear the Sankyo's purr above the crowd.

And the crowd's voice, that large lumpish thing, comes slowly apart in the upper towers of his mind. Bright strands unraveling, flying single and separate, high above the shaping of joyless victory. His kid's name is Carl, or is it Kyle? They want him to G-E-T O-U-T. Mrs. Imbody screams, "Push harder. Wear the turkey down." They're greedy for the fall. But he wants to go on forever, working his skills, flowing from one move to the next, putting off the big moment. . . .

He goes back to the sounds of the gym like one returning to a bothersome thought: a smattering of boos, *stalling on top, stalling on the bottom.* Sure enough. They are chanting *Bobby* and chanting *George.* He listens more closely, goaded by a growing conviction that something vital is missing. He turns his kid with a half. He closes his eyes and lets the word approach again. *Bobby. Bawbee, Bahb-eeee.* It touches him, a tongue probing an old sore. It is suddenly exotic as all names when you really get thinking about them. Strange eruption of sound, this, but only strange; nothing more. Panicked, he looks for the pain, gropes for it. Then the name is swept away in the thundering, pounding, bench-rattling swell of the crowd.

Grief begins at his fingertips and fills him swiftly. What has he lost? What essential nexus? Where has it fled? He is drowning in a sea of English common words rubbed smooth as pebbles. "Bridge, Bobby, bridge!" Mrs. Imbody's voice like a bell through the uproar. He is conscious then of the kid's, Carl or Kyle's, weight across his chest, the desperate downward pressure, his shoulders inching toward the mat.

Overhead light explodes in his eyes. He sees first the ref's arm starting up. It seems to him that he should have some kind of choice in this, but his rights are unclear. The ref is the fine-featured black man. Crouching low, his face dangles like a delicately carved ceremonial mask above the boy's. His smile is a thing apart and alive. Bold, incongruous, teasing him with conjurings of life beyond the death he is about to die: Go down easy, Bobby. Easy now, let it go. Ahhh . . . *Schwack!* Open your eyes, boy. Stand with me. I am real as her scream is real in the morning, real as the seems and the seams of your life. I? I am a moth among the bullfrogs. I am daringly insubstantial, as heedless as your name.

The Johnstown Polka

Francine comes to the doorway of the room where her husband is watching *Lie Detector* and rolling socks from the dark load.

"Let the holey ones set," she says. "I'll darn them later."

Ray does a clownish double take. "Hey, don't *you* look snazzy!"

She is *not* snazzy and knows it. She'd drawn a quick red mouth and combed her hair, is all. She belongs to a group called The Friendly City Singers and tonight they are scheduled up at the rest home again. Good-natured to start with, Ray has been especially helpful since the wire mill shut down. Tonight when he's finished sorting the laundry, and once the kids are rough-housed and bedded down, he'll putz around with the fire company radio set. Francine is glad he signed on with the Jack-Be-Quicks. Other jobless guys keep busy with drinking or barking at their wives all day. "What are you staring at, hon?" asks Ray with a small, wavery smile.

"Nothing," she says. She would never mention the bubble of dullness that routinely drops between her and the faces of her family. She has to look hard then; they could just as well be vaguely familiar strangers she's hard put to place. Brenda and Karen were seven and five when she lost them and their father in the last flood. Her first husband's name was Frank. Frank and Francine, as if they'd been cut from the heart of the same saint. They'd occupied the right half of a double house on Saylor Street. Now this whole wave of new people: big Ray Tomchak with his flat nose and sweet, sleepy expressions. Two more daughters born of pregnancies so easy her body feels unused. The left half of a double on West McBride. She watches as four-year-old Dawn Marie claps Tara under the empty laundry basket. Tara, who is two, sparks and twinkles like a jarred lightning bug. Francine does not have bad dreams about these children. In their dimness and distance, they seem safe enough to her.

Out front her friend Cookie Cannini honks once. Francine dawdles several seconds longer in the archway. The subject on *Lie Detector* is about to have his polygraph read. "It embarrasses me," says Ray, "when F. Lee Bailey has to tell someone they're lying." Francine has a sudden clear picture of herself, haunting her own life, a ghost hanging around to spy on the folks who moved in. She hurries off seconds before the moment of truth.

She is about to open Cookie's car door when she looks back to see Ray bearing down on her, one kid ramrod-style under each arm. "You forgot to kiss us chickens goodbye," he is calling, in a voice close to tears.

Last year, at the firehouse Super Bowl party, Cookie, hoping to recruit Francine for The Friendly City Singers, delivered a little canned speech about "spreading

the notes of hope and cheer among the less fortunate."
"Less fortunate than me?" Francine said too loudly.
"Why, I'd have to run a national hard-luck contest to
find the poor buggers." They both went into hysterics,
throwing the entire bar into embarrassed silence.

"I'm not crazy about performing up at the home,"
Cookie says now. "I mean no amount of songs about
sunshine is liable to snap somebody out of being old."

"But don't people in the cheerin-up business have to
expect some hopeless cases?" Francine winks to show
she's teasing.

"Hey, know that real *real* old one that spits in the
flowerpots? She watches you like a hawk, Francine. With
them little beady eyes."

"Her and me, we got to gabbing some last time. She's
a corker all right. Her name is Libby Quigg. Wears a
badge that says OLDEST LIVING SURVIVOR. City Council
had it made up just for her." Francine neglects to mention how much she is looking forward to seeing the old
woman again.

"Oldest Living Survivor of what?"

"The 1889 flood. Didn't I tell you that?"

"Anymore you never tell me nothing, Francine."

It is February, the haggard month. The night is whit-
ish and gummy. For the first time Francine notices how
stingily lit downtown has become. She watches two delicate baubles of light pass one another on the shadowy
hulk of Westmont Hill. All her life the quaint old cable
cars, long obsolete, have been going up and down, up
and down, keeping a kind of plodding rhythm nobody
in Johnstown seemed willing to surrender. "You ever
ride up the incline, Cook?"

"Nope, not a once in thirty-six years. Isn't that something?"

"New Yorkers probably don't go up on the Statue of Liberty either."

"His Nibs says it's the longest incline plane in the world." Cookie's pet name for her husband Carl is "His Nibs."

"Not the longest, the *steepest*. Hard to believe anybody born and raised in town would bollix up their facts regarding the incline."

"Well, pardon me, Francine Irene!"

Time has tuned their friendship so that it produces not the occasional large, crashing spat but rashes of itchy, picky eruptions. The two women go back a long way; as Cookie is fond of saying, they've been watching each other's perms grow out since grade school. And Francine has kept the acne pits from the years they were both broken out, both round-faced nobodies at Bishop Sweeney High. They wore their school jumpers on the long side and rarely tried to get away with knee socks or colored blouses. To describe the nondescript the yearbook staff resorted to such words as *quiet, pious* and *gentle*. The only activity listed under their pictures was Glee Club 3,4.

At the rest home The Friendly City Singers set up in a stained and sagging lounge so overheated it smells like the presser room at the cleaners. Nobody would dare open a window because old people would gutter and die like candles in a draft. As a rule the singers do the sunshine songs plus "You Light Up My Life," "Singing in the Rain," and a medley of show tunes. Tonight it is from *Fiddler on the Roof*, about as close as you can get to a disaster musical.

She searches among faces that range from sound asleep through indifferent, through hostile, to almost aggressively vivacious. She spots Libby Quigg in a folding chair against the wall, wearing rose-colored waffle-knit polyester pants and a flower barrette. Flanked by two stout aides, she looks under guard, as if she were some museum's very best piece. In the middle of "Sunrise, Sunset" their eyes meet and Libby Quigg winks, making Francine feel the two of them are in cahoots. Oddly pleased and discomfited at the same time, she glances uncertainly toward Cookie, who flattens her final note into a broad, companionable smile.

"You have lipstick on your tooth," Francine whispers.

Cookie swipes a wrist across her bridgework and then Aggie Wojnoroski bounds out with the accordion, plants her feet far apart and strikes up the lead-in to "The Johnstown Polka." It is something of a sign-off number and they can always get a handful of live wires to do a few stomping turns around the room, accompanied by a lot of clapping and whooping and some occasional grumbling about old fools.

Afterward the home always provides light refreshments. Tonight there is a beverage and butter cookies on a Ping-Pong table spread with a birthday cloth and matching paper napkins. Francine takes two Lorna Doones and ladles purple Kool-Aid for herself, then fills several other cups held out to her. One is attached to Libby Quigg. "Don't yis know no snappy numbers?" she asks.

Francine smiles. Next to the withered creature, she sees herself as benignly huge, floating, a balloon Petunia Pig. "Anybody's got a request, they can drop it in the suggestion box we pass around." It has not escaped her how deftly Libby Quigg is stuffing her pockets with free cookies.

The old woman squints, studying Francine. "Where do you live anyways?"

"A little piece from here. Down closer to town."

She pokes Francine in the forearm and leans close. "We got take-out here," she whispers.

"I don't see no lunch counter. Take-out what?"

"Only item we got. Old-timers like me."

Francine stares down and Libby Quigg adds confidentially, "As you say, Missy, ain't no picnic lookin at them gummers all day." Then before Francine can reply, she whistles through two fingers and one of the heavyset aides hustles over, buxom, open-faced, ruddily cheerful.

"Riley, this here lady's askin after that there new program."

Riley thinks. "Oh, you mean our Foster Grandpersons program. Well, now I can't imagine which of our many deserving residents we're talking about here," she teases, securing the sliding barrette.

Francine looks hard at the old woman, all bone and blue veins, bituminous eyes bright, her proud badge festooned with a faded blue ribbon: She might be first prize in an antique-doll contest, the kind of doll too fragile to touch. "You'd let her go off with just—anybody?"

"Mercy, no. Not just anybody. Interested parties have

to be screened and approved by our director."

"Just so's you're clean and keep a Christian tongue in your mouth."

"Libby," says Riley, "you're a piece of work."

As one of the heavy losers in what they now call Flood '77, Francine was, for a short time, famous. Lately, people shyly compliment her on how she's "come to terms" and call her a trooper. But what they perceive as tranquillity, Francine experiences as a sort of unpleasant limpness, her heart a slack muscle, as if after having delivered an outsized grief, it never quite snapped back and stubbornly holds, if not sorrow itself, then the soft shape of it. Fearing the worst always made the best moments better, pulled them snug and taut. Now that the worst has happened the world is at least a size too big, and she is loose in her skin, at large in time.

Oddly enough—and Ray says it's the Slovenian peasant in her—the one thing she is afraid of is starving. Against this possibility, she is fortunate to have a part-time job, four mornings a week, at Kloibers' lingerie department. "Have you Kloibered today?" reads the Easy Grade billboard. The store smells of redskin peanuts and something faintly fishy that Francine has convinced herself is a chemical they add to merchandise so you know it's cheap.

After a slow start the morning begins. Two elevators discharge a flutter of noisy women with smudged foreheads. Ash Wednesday services at Saint John's has just let out. The women surround the tables where winter clearance items lie in soft, vaguely disreputable piles;

they rummage without pushiness or hurry, for there is plenty left this year. In mantillas and rayon babushkas they chat and laugh, hold pajama tops against the bosoms of strangers shaped similarly to mothers and daughters, making Francine recall almost happily why the town is called The Friendly City. This morning the voices carry a bright overlay of excitement. "What's going on?" Francine asks someone when she hears the name Morley Safer bobbing up out of the conversations again and again.

"Why, the *Sixty Minutes* crew is down setting up in the park. Mr. Safer wants us to stop down after bit, to get interviewed. And me dressed like a big bum!" The woman is wearing a black satin jacket that says CAMBRIA COUNTY ALL STARS—168 POUNDER. "My Stanley's wrastling coat. I sure wasn't planning on bumping into nobody famous."

Two women approach the check-out. One of them dumps an armload of large pink underpants on the counter, taps Francine delicately on the elbow. "Beg pardon, Miss, but isn't Gene Kelly a Johnstown boy?"

Francine says, "I always heard he comes from Pittsburgh, Ma'm."

"I told you, Floss. That was his sister run the dance studio on Main Street." The second woman wears a lapel pin that says POLSKI POWER.

"Well, Bea, then that leaves us with Carroll Baker and Johnny Weismuller."

"Strictly speaking," Francine interjects, "Weismuller was more from Windber—better check them pants for flaws, Ma'm."

The soiled foreheads call to mind something Francine heard back in grade school, that removing the ashes was the same as wiping off the Savior's kiss. Thus warned, she kept adding coal ashes from the school boiler room. Now she doesn't go to church at all except maybe from time to time when Cookie gets it into her head to run down to Saint Basil's for the guitar Mass. Lately Ray's been studying with a nice Jehovah's Witness couple who started coming around about the time of the heaviest layoffs. They are living in the Last Days, Ray insists. The hard times will give way to something called the New System. "This is not your basic heaven thing," he is careful to point out. Then he tries to explain how Francine can look forward to reunion with *all* her loved ones in a place that sounds suspiciously to her like the same old planet, the same old grubby mill town. "Now what kind of goofball would sign up for a deal like that?" she'd said, confusing him so he could not reply. But from some dim fifties classroom inside her a hand shot up and a child's voice, small but rushingly hopeful cried, *Me! Oh, me. Oh, I will!*

When the worst of the midmorning rush is past and the customers have started downstairs to pursue stardom in the park, Francine sets aside a flannel nightgown reduced to $3.49 because she can picture Libby Quigg in it.

Francine is doing her food shopping in the supermarket section of Kloiber Brothers, where she has a choice of using her employee discount or double coupons. Tara rides in the cart while Dawn Marie skips alongside. Earlier, out front, she caught a glimpse of the morning's headlines in the window of the newspaper machine: IT'S OFFICIAL: JOHNSTOWN HOME OF NATION'S HIGHEST UNEMPLOYMENT. The letters were inky and boastful and made her very hungry.

It amazes her now to see what she's heaped into the cart without thinking. Italian-cut veal, fresh scallops, grapes, persimmons, three kinds of Pop-Tarts . . . and Tara tossing on top, with joyful abandon, a half dozen Ring Ding Jr.'s. Francine lifts her out of the seat. She tries to stand her upright next to Dawn Marie, at which point the child goes off like some hair-trigger, fiendishly shrill alarm. She draws up her legs, making herself a dead weight, as heavy as two small girls, three, four; Francine feels she could snap from the weight of so many youngsters hanging from her branches, and still they do not reach the ground.

Weepy and confused, she phones Ray and he gets a neighbor to run him over to Kloibers'. He takes the baby to the drugstore for a Slurpy while Francine and Dawn Marie return everything to the shelves but what she came for, plus an econo-pak of chicken legs on special. The Muzak system, which has been piping a seamless ribbon of old smoothies that makes her feel, annoyingly, like skating in the aisles, stops short, pauses, and starts pumping out the *tompa, tompa, tompa* of "The Johnstown Polka." Dawn Marie whirls around the cart in a dance that resembles someone stamping out small grass fires.

That night, Francine is kept awake by the thump of words and music in her head. *Let's play the Johnstown Polka, for the city with a will. Let's play the Johnstown Polka, the city that floodwaters couldn't kill.* To keep the beat it is necessary to rush the word *floodwaters*. When Francine was a girl she always thought the song went: "the city that *Bud Walters* couldn't kill."

Back then, the last thing people worried over was another trial by water. Like smallpox and polio, floods were considered a threat of some dim and savage past, magnanimously vanquished by none other than FDR. After the flood in '36 it was Roosevelt who put the army engineers to work on the river, and when they were through he dedicated the handsome floodwalls himself. Francine always pictured a frail, fatherly figure scribing a benediction over darkish waters, while somewhere in the depths of the city set in a hole in the mountains skulked a gent named Bud Walters, wearing shiny brown waders and hatching plots.

"The floods were all different!" she says aloud at 3:05 A.M., her voice glittery with discovery and indignation.

Ray comes noisily unstuck from sleep. "Wha' happened?"

"Those dumb old walls didn't mean a thing, Ray." She says this as if pointing up some hypocrisy he had personally to answer for. "Except for thirty-six the river never even got a chance to rise. In 1889 it was a busted dam wrecked up the place. In *my* flood it rained like crazy, water poured off the hills, and the town filled up like a cup of filthy tea."

His large hand paws her breast in an ungainly measure of love and helplessness. Sometimes it's hard to remember this bear of a man is Cookie's little brother. "Let's move," he says thickly. "Want to go someplace where it's nice year round?"

A sudden vision of this proposed peaceable kingdom makes her unexpectedly queasy. "No!" she snaps, thinking at the same time how she would never have left Frank Suttmiller either, bullyish and mean-tempered as he got occasionally. Once he whipped a safety razor at her, chipping her collarbone. It was the tough-knuckled stuff that held you. What the yearbook staff said about Francine was: "She'll gently steal your heart away." All that meant was nobody knew she was alive.

Sunday night. Rain drumming on the flat roof of the Jack-Be-Quick firehouse. Ray has drawn bartending duty this weekend and Francine sits next to Cookie at the nearly deserted bar. Francine's second wedding reception was held here and the first one took place in a similar firehall out in Holsopple. The weddings slosh together in a slather of French dressing, baked ziti, and spilt beer. Both times a rowdy bunch drove her and the groom thrice around the block in the back of a screaming red pumper. It is possible to believe she died in '77 and came back as the same person. Of course she didn't marry Ray in white. She wore instead something buff-colored borrowed from Cookie. It was cut in a princess line with a bolero jacket, a little slack across the bust.

Francine dips a pretzel in mustard and sits back, sipping Iron City draft and waiting for *60 Minutes* to start. For some reason it does not seem surprising to her that the show opens with a profile shot of Miss Libby Quigg in a high-backed rocker. Cookie is beside herself. "Look, it's that flood lady!" she cries.

"Trick photography," says His Nibs, explaining how it so happens you can see right through Miss Quigg's body to the dark background shapes of smokestacks and mountains. The voice-over identifies her briefly, calling her a living testimonial to some high-sounding notion Francine doesn't quite follow. Then polka music kicks in, the focus solidifies, and Safer steps into the picture, extends a courtly hand and asks Miss Quigg to dance.

Cookie says, "I bet they had to cut out the part where she spits in the fern." Francine has to laugh, especially when she thinks how she'd just today arranged with the rest home director to take the spitting fool for one overnight. Why Francine wants to do this she can't imagine.

Some people Francine does not know come on now, relating what Ray calls "heart-rendering tales." Then she sees the woman in the black satin jacket, looking sheepish as the camera zooms in on the sharp white wrestling figure over her breast. In the middle of a sentence she stops short, crossing her arms determinedly high. "Hey," she says almost crossly, "we have to live in our lives, Mister. Same as you, Mister!" Francine looks close but cannot tell if the ash smudge is still there.

There follows a sequence featuring Mayor Popp, hatless and fit-looking as he strolls with Safer in a wind that makes a noise like bronchitis in the mike. "Darndest thing, Morley," he says, letting on like the two of them are old friends. "The economic picture around here might look a little hairy, but son of a gun, that old crime rate keeps coming down. Johnstown's a darn safe place to live."

A swell of pride makes Francine feel bloated and foolish, so she says, "Son of a gun, Morley, Kloibers'

Santa Claus got busted for shoplifting."

"Shhhh," says Cookie. "Isn't that Ziggy and Joan Yuhas?"

The segment ends with Safer riding up on the incline, scarf whipping, his clean blade of commercial baritone paring them down to a moral: "This tough little Pennsylvania town the rest of us would do well to remember next time we're tempted to grumble about the weather or the price of bridge mix."

"Well, I think that was real nice," someone says at the break. "What the heck is bridge mix?" The next story is about a ring of frozen-food hijackers working out of Shreveport.

"Oh, before I forget . . ." Cookie digs in her handbag. "I picked up these refund forms for you at the Shop 'N Save. A Birds Eye Orientals and a Head and Shoulders."

"I don't have dandruff," says Francine, and Cookie looks crestfallen. Cookie likes to think they're twins. They should both have dandruff. Once she said, "Isn't *Laverne and Shirley* you and me all over again?"

Francine can't see this. They'd never pulled harebrained or scary stunts. The worst thing she remembers is the time they wrote WASH ME on the convent station wagon. In terms of Lucy and Ethel, they were more like Ethel and Ethel.

"I cut out some coupons for you," she says, "but didn't I go and forget them."

His Nibs never sits with the women but stands up by the TV with Ray. The two of them crack up over something; then Ray comes down toward the women carrying the joke in his mouth. It's for her, Francine. He will feed her fun and laughter and drown out the sound of the rain.

So prim and subdued is Libby Quigg at supper that Francine imagines the home has a policy of drugging its clients to keep them from acting up when they're out. The children steal glances, grow bolder. At last Libby Quigg looks up from her plate, fixing Dawn Marie fiercely. "See here, Missy, once I was young as your mum and not half so plain." When Francine passes the tossed salad, she snaps, "I'd sooner have slaw." She takes three helpings of strawberry junket. Her greed and bad manners throw the children into raptures of glee.

At bedtime, when she demands a Mr. Bubble bath, Ray helps get her in and out of the tub, trying hard not to peek. Miss Quigg's flesh looks as if it's been steeping in brine for years; her breasts melt away in drips and squiggles. Then Francine dresses her in the Kloibers' nightgown and paints the horny yellow fingernails with rainbow sparkles.

Later, sleeping next to Ray on the sofa bed, she dreams that she is walking down the aisle of a trolley as it approaches her street. Unaccountably, the contents of her pocketbook begin to fall on the floor. As quickly as she can recover things—a button, a spatula, a chalk-ware chicken—others drop out. She pursues marbles and jawbreakers under the seats. The process is endless, impossible. Looking out the window, she sees that it is not her stop after all. She has never seen this neigh-borhood before.

Francine wakes all knotted up and her heart hurts. The dream lingers, lays in all her hollows, but as soon as she can grope free of it, she rises and puts on her slippers and climbs the narrow staircase to see if the old woman is still breathing.

"I figgered you'd show up." The brassy tones spinning out of the dark startle Francine. She has never had a secret lover, but meeting a man might be like this, touchy, dangerous, her skin prickling.

"I knowed from the first who you are. I seen your pitcher in the paper."

"You did?" Francine is obliquely disappointed. She'd imagined a special telepathy between them, some rare communion of victims across time. She'd almost forgotten about the article, how the reporter held her hand as she talked and the soft sound of the tape recorder munching on her pain.

"Tell me again the part where your hubby says 'The house is about to shift, Toots.' "

Nobody says *Toots* anymore. Nobody asks her these things. Who would have the nerve? "You mean when we were all up setting on the bed?"

"I believe that's the part. Yep."

"What can I say, Miss Libby? We had the kids between us. We were listening to the rain, hoping the water wouldn't rise no more—it was already past the stair landing. Just after Frank said that, there was a horrible crunching sound and we had to just set there and watch the bathroom split apart. And then the bedroom. "Ride with it," he says and then everything was flying and me trying to grab hold of everybody at once. *'Don't let go!'* one of my girls yelled above the racket. For a second, you know, it was just like we was at the tippy top of the

Hershey Park Coaster." Her lips go dry; her mouth sticks, stops.

Libby Quigg huffs impatiently. "Then what?"

"Then something whacked me across the head and back and well, I hardly remember—from being stunned and all."

The old woman pops up in bed. Her voice is like gristle. "You let go of them youngsters, that's what."

Francine tries to ignore the remark. "The coroner came to see me in the hospital. 'Your husband have a missing fingertip?' he wanted to know. 'Your children wear underpants with stars on them?'" Moonlight pushing under the drawn shades sets the nail sparkles aglitter. "Still and all," says Libby Quigg, "as floods go, yours don't amount to beans."

Francine's voice is calm as deepest cold. "No," says she. "It wasn't near so bad as eighty-nine."

"Wanna hear about the *real* flood?"

Francine sits down on the edge of the bed, demurely, innocently, head bowed. As if her heart weren't thundering like ten hearts, as if she had nothing to fear from these details, nothing to gain.

Libby Quigg pinches Francine's thigh. "As you say, Missy, when I'm dang good and ready, mebbe I'll tell you." Then she squeezes crepey eyelids shut and starts to snore.

Francine feels like a fool. "Faker!" she says huskily. "I was plannin on taking you up the incline next week. But why should I do anything for some old meanie who isn't even no relation of mine."

Libby Quigg opens one eye. "Can I at least have a

churry pop to take home with me?" And Francine says, "We'll see."

Several days later Riley telephones to remind Francine she promised—*promised*—Libby Quigg a trip up the incline. Francine can hear the old woman's voice prompting in the background. Shoot, she thinks, but isn't Libby the pisser. Bull-headed, bossy, a little tetched to boot. A scrap on the sleeve of the living. And it's starting to look like Francine is stuck with her. "Riley," she says, "That old lady gets a heck of a kick out of herself."

It has not occurred to Francine to ask if the rushing air might be too much for Libby Quigg. She cannot conceive of harm in air, air flapping around you like a light coat. But the inclined plane operator tries to lead Miss Quigg toward the rear of the car, which is more sheltered. His arm moves easily around the small sloped shoulders, a natural gesture, thinks Francine, in a city of oldsters. It is rare anymore that new people move into town. Most residents have been here for years and how the generations pile up, on the same street, in the same house. Grandmothers are a prized lot, kept out of the cold, in pink sweaters. "Back up a bit, Mom," the boy is saying gently.

By way of reply, Libby Quigg tightens a two-fisted grip on the metal tailgate. The car starts to climb, and Francine imagines herself and Libby as passengers at the windy railing of the Love Boat, fog boiling around them, glazed salmon and whole lobsters waiting below deck. She wishes she'd thought to bring a small snack.

Pulleys tug them higher and higher. The town spreads

out, low-slung and numb-looking under graphite skies. Churches everywhere, craning out of the valley, tucked into the hills and ridges, the tandem spires of Saint Joe's and Saint John's. Down by the stadium, the metallic wishbone formed by three frozen rivers. It shocks her now to see how unbothered the skies are, just a few sickly-yellow plumes when years ago you were hard pressed to find any sky at all through coils of smoke and fumes. And if you stood on Prospect Hill when they opened the blast furnaces you would witness the heavens turn all the gorgeous shades of hell. And practically everyone she knows has a relative who's fallen into a vat of molten steel and been rolled, pulled, or molded into something useful.

At the top it is already snowing. "Down, please," she says, politely, just as if she were in Kloibers' elevator. The smooth descent makes her stomach rise and when she looks down she cannot find where the land falls away beneath them. "Oh, it *is* steep," she says to nobody, for Libby Quigg has thrust her head out and is trying to spit against the airstream.

The old woman refuses to disembark at the base station. "*No*sir!" she says.

"Well, all right," Francine says uncertainly. "One more time."

By their second descent snow is coming in furious funnels. The tumultuous air makes Francine feel up-ended and a little dizzy. Seeing the terminal approach, Libby Quigg says, "One more time. You *promised!*"

"Stop saying that! I should know what I promised."

"Tell you about the Big Flood, hope to die!"

"But I'm cold, aren't you?" The word *cold* cracks her

voice into an ugly whine. But fearing the old woman's gift for guff, sighing, Francine shells out another dollar. Then she draws Libby Quigg back from the open air. "At least talk where I can hear you good."

"Okay, okay. Can I borry a hanky first?" Francine shoves a crumpled tissue into her hand. When Libby Quigg is finished blowing her nose, she stabs a sudden finger at the heart of town. "We lived down there," she says. "One-oh-two Jackson. I was hiding in the attic when my papa called. Course I didn't pay him no mind. That was my way, back then."

"Then?" says Francine under her breath. "That's a laugh!"

"My papa called and called and 'fore long I saw him out my window with Mama and Brother running to beat the band across the backyards." She pitters her chest, out of breath herself.

"Way-el," she continues, "just about the same time I hear a turrible, *turrible* sound, like a train roarin up from Franklin. At first sight it didn't look like nothing but a big wall of dust—later, folks would call it the "devil mist"—mebbe fifty foot tall at the middle." She makes a careless gesture into the distance and Francine catches herself squinting hard, as if she might make out such a wonder looming high above the bleary rooftops. "How old were you then?" she asks.

"Near seven. And clever for my age!" She gives an abrupt nod. "Now, as you say, anything got in the path of that wave was a goner. Why, Saint John's steeple busted off like a icicle. When it come closer I could see— not water; no, you couldn't see no water t'all—just this mountain of stuff, coal cars, rooftops, chimleys, dead cows, church pews. It was such a stupefyin sight I almost forgot to be askeared, till it hit. Why, that there fine house rockered back and forth just like a tooth bein yanked." She pauses importantly, jabs a finger in Francine's ribs. "Think of it, Missy! Then all of a sudden them walls just split and the floorboards broke upwards, all jagged and hoorible. I was afalling. . ."

As in a dream of falling, Francine feels her body jerk. Instinctively, she reaches out to grab the old woman's elbow, and when she does Libby Quigg clamps her mouth shut and draws an imaginary zipper across her lips.

Francine says, "You got money to get back if I don't pay the fare?"

Libby Quigg thinks this over. "Oh, all right," she huffs. "As you say, next thing I'm hightailin it across town on a mattress. I yelled to a young fella tryin to keep his balance on top of a B and O caboose, but he just went his merry way. Solly, the iceman, and his family sweeps by on a big wood floor. My, my, but they was busy beavers, packin all their belongins in a little Saratoga trunk. Next second the whole bunch got crushed under that there caboose. A half-nekked fella come by on a pitched roof. He waved and I waved and then he was gone."

Almost absently Francine tucks a few strands of fine hair into Libby Quigg's hat. The old woman squirms against her pleasure. "Pay attention now," she says sternly. "I led an excitin life up till now."

"I'm not going nowhere, Miss Libby."

"Way-el, soon I was floating along real calm on a cellar door I hooked up with a way back. But just when I started lookin for a place to drop anchor, so to speak, the current slammed into the mountainside and there I was, ashootin back the way I come."

Francine gapes incredulously. She shakes her head. Then it comes to her that this is the part toward which she's been steering from the very start. It's the question she has to ask even though somehow she has known the answer since the first time she laid eyes on Libby Quigg. Francine straightens her shoulders and unravels a long breath. "And the family—your papa and them. They—did they—everybody made it to high ground?"

"The dickens they did. They was carried all the way down the crick to the Loyalhanna. And Mama—why, they didn't find Mama t'all. People up on Benschoff Hill took me in and brung me up proper."

There is an instant of perfect white quiet before Francine is taken with craziness. A red hot rush rope-burns her spine; the base of her brain is burning. She clenches and unclenches her fist and then her fingers fly out and take a fearsome grip on Libby Quigg. She digs her nails, presses so hard the tension trembles the old shoulders. Black and canny, Libby's eyes blaze back at her. Francine is wild to speak it. Speak what? The words that say rage and pain and forever are swept like minnows, like grains of sand—like children—into the mouth of God. Everything in Francine's world is either too large or too small. "I . . . ," she starts. "G-god . . ."

"Well, spit it out!" says Libby Quigg.

"You!" she says finally, fiercely. "Shame on you! You make that flood sound like the circus come to town, like you was just havin yourself a ball."

The old woman sniffs and shoves out her lower lip. "So what if I was?" she says coyly. "What if I was?" Daring Francine to make something of it.

With a sudden jerk Francine hitches Libby close to her side, tugs her front and around until they are both belly against the tailgate. "Hey!" squeals Libby in protest. Francine makes another fist and holds it under her mouth like a microphone. She's about as far as she's ever been from quiet and pious and gentle. "Hey!" she hollers into raging white space. "Mind your own business, Mister!" Libby giggles into her sleeve. Staring down at her, Francine blinks and blinks, breathing very fast and very hard.

They are heading down now for the last time. The *very* last time, Francine has informed the very old child. Watery supper hour lights show through the cold curtain. "Hungry?" she asks. Libby says, "Yup." The car is plunging, rocking into the wind. Libby's hand is cold and smooth as mother-of-pearl. Houses with lighted porches rush up at them and Francine leans out looking hard for one house, half a house, set deep in a teacup town filling fast with snow

Heart of the Dutch Country

"Isn't he the perfect hayseed!" My mother's eyes are shining the way they do when she goes glittery inside and the light comes splashing up out of her. Even her face glows, spotty, like there's a tiny pink bulb burning behind each cheek. She lets on like it's all a big tease, like she's giving Caffrey the business, but you know better; it's just her way of making us all party to her pleasure. The perfect hayseed! She'd gush if he was the perfect pissant.

She's right though. She made Caff wear Dad's good patchwork shirt and Little Chip supplied the wide striped suspenders and the broad-brimmed sun hat. His thatchy hair is bleached lighter than the straw of his hat, and he's tall, muscular from two wrestling seasons. So he looks like a pig farmer. Big whoop.

It's a wonder Caffrey even got the job; he takes forever getting around to things. Months before the festival I had mine nailed down. Fact is Mr. Bittner called *me*. After three years I have a kind of tenure. But good old daydreaming, air-headed Caffrey goes biking down to the fairgrounds just two days before the opening, and the best he can come up with is a maybe from Little Chip. And believe me, Little Chip is the worst he could come up with. Works your can off and pays ninety bucks for a full week of twelve-hour days. Of course, I can just hear Caff: *Excuse me, sir, you wouldn't still be hiring, would you? Probably got all the help you need, right?* Then when the guy asked his age, he'd have told him fifteen, when everyone knows he doesn't care if you're nine as long as you say sixteen. It's a well-known fact anyhow that Little Chip prefers teenyboppers because they don't rip him off as bad as us older, hardened types. When Little Chip called that night, you'd have thought Caff had just won half of downtown Reading instead of a chance to give vacationing America a three-day heartburn.

The perfect hayseed! She wouldn't call *me* that. I heard her griping to Mrs. Rabenold one day about my "pretty girl complex," but even that was just a big sneaky brag. On this, the fourth morning of the eighteenth annual Kecktown Pennsylvania Dutch Folk Festival, I am in blue-and-white gingham with a matching Amish sunbonnet. I have my brother's yellow hair, but mine is finer and shinier. I've been letting it grow and it's just below my shoulders. Yesterday this couple with pokey Texas tongues came by. The lady elbowed the man, nodding toward me like I was part of the agricultural exhibit: "There's your classic bucolic." And out came his Nikon. That's me. Early milkmaid. But Mom just says, "Don't you think the gym shoes confuse the image?"

Not that she dotes on Caffrey more. I just don't let her get away with those long, sipping looks, the way she seems to take nourishment from our persons. We're an unremarkable pair, from the fattest part of the bell-shaped curve, but she's got every bone of our bodies set to music. She's always staring, tuned in like she's recording something that'll never be played again. Now

181

she's got Caffrey smiling self-consciously. *Ah, shucks, Ma'm!* Bet she's got the serrated edges of his teeth counted.

Then Caffrey gives the hayseed stuff and her absorbent gaze a couple more here-and-gone grins and the old wipe-the-side-of-the-nose routine. He's too nice to roll his eyes back the way I do or stare the stickiness out of her eyes.

That's his trouble and that's her trouble, and maybe that's why there is, after all, something special between them: They're a matching set. There's a slowness there—a *flowness* actually. They're like rivers lapping calmly along in the dead of summer, unbothered by the fact that six smart-ass dudes on the bank are chucking Yoo-Hoo bottles at them. Well, you could just shake them. Especially when you're waiting around some boring department store and the clerk says, can I help you, and they look up like they've been asleep a hundred years and say something like—"Uh, do you handle . . . uh, does the store sell . . . uh . . . ?" and I've got to prompt and fill in *greeting cards* or *ice-cream makers* or whatever. Dad always said their minds were out raking hay, which is not to say we're farmers. Let's be clear on that. This whole rustic scene is starting to get to me like it does this time every year. Dad was a trial lawyer before he died last spring, and we're certainly not Pennsylvania Dutch just because we happen to be living, as they say, in the heart of the Dutch country.

But you do have to wonder what those two think about when they're putting scissors in the refrigerator and milk in the broom closet. In one month alone Mom left the Plaza Shopping Center three times with her groceries sitting in the cart in front of Thrift Drugs. She figures it out when she gets home and there's nothing to put away. Caff's worldly goods are spread out over three counties but he couldn't tell you who's got what, and I owe him a ten-spot he's long forgotten.

Studied ineptitude, Dad used to call it. But he was wrong about the studied part; they're both naturals. Saturday night Caff'll get his festival pay and by Tuesday morning already he'll be hitting Mom for pocket money, and she'll fork it over, marveling at his largeness of spirit and, at the same time, commending me for being tough and independent and thrifty because I've still got mine—every last nickel.

"Let's get bookin'," I tell Caffrey. "Scrooge Mc-Bittner lays eggs if we're ten seconds late." But naturally old Caff left his pocket calculator upstairs and goes loping down the hallway in giant, slow-motion strides. Flowing along.

Mom walks out to the Volks with me. She thinks Caffrey's using his calculator on the job shows he's "finally acquired a little, uh, initiative, not to mention a budding talent for uh, organization." And I must admit, it's uncaffreylike. She's standing in front of the rose garden—not much now in early July—pulling her hair out. Thinks she's going bald, so she hurries things along with this revolting habit of raking with her fingers, then checking her hand for the take. Her fingers flutter apart, letting two or three long metallic strands float lazily to the macadam.

"That grosses me out," I groan, turning away. And when I look back, I am stung again by how age can fly from her in a second and how her child's face guards

such secrets and shuttered rooms. Who *are* you? I want
to shout to her shell of bruised softness, but Caffrey has
come out. About to climb into our little red convertible,
he sees her injuries. (They're like that, both of them.)
He kisses her cheek and says, "Have a good day, Lydia
Pinkham." In the process his straw hat tips off. He picks
it up and glances quickly at Mom's beetle-bitten Crim-
son Glories; looks back at his unicycle leaning against
the house. Excitement livens his face, but there's also
that questioning look people get when they can't remember what they forgot. I say, "Get your butt in gear,
man, and let's go."

It's going to be a stinker of a day. Motionless. Sun's
doing a slow yellow burn behind a grayish scum sky.
All the way to Kecktown, Caffrey "entertains." He's im-
provising this corny Nazi Cooking School routine that
I'm trying to ignore till I hear him say: "A German
kuchen, madame? Nein, nein, ve·do not lay da apple
slices carefully in rows. Ve dump dem on top of cake,
like so. Den ve hollah, *'Achtung!'* und dey all line up." I
have to smile—can't help it. It's a tricky thing: He can
really crack you up, but you can't encourage him or he'll
keep grinding it out forever. And I just want some peace
and quiet before getting back in character.

Much as I hate to admit it though, show biz is starting to pay off for him. I work at Hex Jewelry at the
upper end of The General Store, one of several per-
manent exhibit buildings on the grounds. His stand is
directly across from the entranceway. It's called Dutch
Stuff For To Eat. Little Chip started him out on the grill,
sweating over sausages and fried peppers. Well, he
couldn't just drudge down and shut up. Half an hour

later I could hear him—low key at first, a little shy—starting to pitch the disgusting stuff: "Farm-fresh sausages. Get your sausages here."

I took the early break that day and slipped over to freeload a bite. By then he was grinding out jingles as fast as he could dream them up, which was pretty freakin' fast. Sausage songs and fritter songs. Snappy little rhymes about how cider will delight her. "Get your sausage hot or sweet, get your Dutch stuff for to eat!" And I had to wait in line. Next to me a lady chirped to her companion, "These folk seem to retain a kind of elemental *joie de vivre.*" Then the little scuzz wanted to charge me, his own sister, including tax. Now a lot of kids make extra bucks from what they can lift out of the cash boxes; I wouldn't touch a nickel. But no way am I coughing up a buck-fifty for a "waffel mit lemon drinka." None of us kids actually *charge* each other. The little stupe! So he said, okay, he'd take care of it, and damned if he didn't take a buck and a half out of his pocket and drop it in the box. The thing is he was having himself a blast bopping around back there, charming the pants off the mob. And when good ole Little Chip, the kingpin of the local munchies set, came by, he was grinning so wide the cigar fell out of his mouth. He picked it up, wiped it on the seat of his pants and replaced it with fingers fat and brown as his Lebanon County sausages.

Well, as I said, all it takes to really get Caff going is a little audience response. By the next day he was really giving them what they wanted: Howard Cosell in a play-by-play broadcast of the making of a funnel cake; John Wayne talking up indigestion: "Let me tell ya, Pilgrim,

if you've got a hankerin' for a real fine fritter . . ."
Jimmy Cagney and Jimmy Stewart, and all day, each
time I ran over, the routines kept getting more elabo-
rate. Mr. Joie de Vivre! The round and doughy ladies
in the back had to hustle to keep the goodies coming to
the counter. They chuckled cheekily among themselves. Caffrey was off the grill forever. Every once in
a while thin ripples of applause drifted across to Hex
Jewelry.

Last night Caff told me that Little Chip was making
him his No. 2 man, and, wonder of wonders, promised
him a 10 percent cut of all proceeds over and above the
average daily take, whatever that means. I told him if
he believed that derelict, he was even dumber than I
thought. Caff looked at me with those big inky blue eyes
I should have gotten (mine are the color of canned
mushrooms) and said, "Well, why would he lie?" There's
no getting through to a gullible nin like Caffrey. Let
him think Little Chip is going to make him a star.

We have to park way down by the Shaffer Street gate
because half the ever-lovin' country has already shown
up. Caff hops out of the car, does a loose little shuffle
step. "Um-um," he grunts in his black boy's voice, "it be
a big day fo' us puhveyahs of frittahs and frahd sausage." Tossing his hat before him, he does a hand-
spring between cars and scrambles up the bank to the
lower end of the grounds. I curse a lot because I have
to walk so far today and my skirt is too long.

He waits for me up in front of the Funeral Lore tent,
by the big polished horse-drawn hearse. It's the last exhibit on "lore lane." Years ago I went in there with Mom
and Dad. I remember mostly how the heat swallowed

you from the shoulders up: all that hot stale air trapped under the black canvas. Nobody seemed to breathe; they'd gaze silently at six-sided Mennonite coffins and old embalming tables, the row of infant caskets, drawn back somehow like people peering out over a steep ravine. And the odor. Only recently I discovered that what I've grown up to think of as "the stench of death" is really just the smell of corn being ground into flour at the adjacent Gristmill Lore. Still, there it lay—dry and flat and powdery in my nostrils—the night of Dad's viewing, blotting up the air and the bitter smell of chrysanthemums and painted daisies.

We hurry on down through the "lores." This year they've added a few new ones: Decoy Lore, Sheepskin Lore, Puzzle Lore, Painting-on-Velvet Lore. At the potter we stop for a second and wave to a guy wedging a hunk of red clay. He's Mr. Fugue, who's really a physics teacher at our school. A few years ago, when I was ten and Caff nine, he came up to talk to Dad about his daughter's automobile accident. At dinner he was telling us she'd needed 126 stitches and how an artery had popped like a spring right out of her head. Well, Caff must have been chewing on that one because after a while these words came out from under his milk mustache: "God's like a kid with too many toys to take care of, isn't he?" We don't go to church, so I've always been stuck with the gospel according to Caff.

Already the barrel maker's coopering, the glass blower blowing, the herbalist tying up dried flowers and islands of sweat are spreading under his arms. They're starting up the ancient gas engines, and the air begins to choke and sputter and belch with their laboring to

187

drive mile-long belts attached to saws and threshers and post-hole drillers. The first tendrils of smoke come up from kettles and boilers and blacksmith's fires. Down here the festival smells are hard-working, no-nonsense: beeswax, lye soap, ash and hickory. We reach the tiny white church. Inside, Mrs. Shenfelder is already leading some tourists in a chorus of "Shall We Gather by the River." I poke my head in the window. The people look huge, like they've grown too big for the building; their heads nearly touch the ceiling. "Come on," he says, "I'm going to be late."

"Huh?" I say. Caffrey never hustled his butt for anybody! He says, "See ya later," and cuts through the little graveyard next to the little church and disappears around the little tavern behind which the food and drink stands start and the grease-and-onion air I'll be sucking up all day.

Right off, Mr. Bittner gives my Adidas the once over. "No sneakers," he says. I reply almost sweetly, "Then you can take care of my shin splints and pay for the knee operation." I point to the cement floor. A funny wet rattle comes out of his pouchy throat. He lets me alone then, mainly because the phrase *pay for* strikes a responsive note, but also because I can get away with a lot—a fact of life that comes with the Complex.

Not that he really gives a damn what we wear, but sometimes the festival officials come by with this spiel about keeping the festival authentic. Hokey and homespun and all that. And Bittner's not about to lose this space.

Now he's back again, wants me to get rid of the cardboard cartons our "handcrafted" copper horse-and-buggies came in, P.D.Q. Seems somebody noticed the Made-in-Taiwan stamp. Bittner says it's not a matter of taking people at all but of giving them what they want—which is to be taken, royally. Once he told me in this great, quaking, prophetic voice that given a choice, most people will pick the "cutesy poo" and the phony over the genuine. "You see," he said, "it eliminates that light brush with truth that could threaten the very ground they walk on. . . ." "My, my," I said, "behold the Philosopher General."

Well, much as I can't stand the strutting fool, he's got a point, the way they come through here knocking each other down to get at this schlock. Somebody came up with HEART OF THE DUTCH COUNTRY for this year: white letters on a big red heart. And everybody freaked out, like little kids with a new dirty word. It's plastered on everything: T-shirts and pennants, mugs and jugs, sand buckets and berry buckets and miniature washtubs. This year they've added Moo Moo Creamers to the line and we can't keep them in stock.

Around ten I'm dying of thirst. Last night I told Caffrey to get something cold and wet to me when he gets his break, since I have the late one today. It's clear, though, when I look over, that breaking is the furthest thing from his mind. This early in the day, and he's already got a following, literally eating out of his hand. I try to grab his attention, but Little Chip's got him by the arm. Caff's bending low to give old cigar-breath his ear. I imagine Little Chip to be saying: *Kid, you're knocking them dead.* At the same time Caffrey dips smoothly, sliding something down the counter.

Round and round my head it plays, *kid you're knocking them dead, oh, kid, you're knocking them dead,* and while I set out a section of charms, that scene's stop-actioned in my brain: Caffrey and the great L.C., Partners for all time, co-designers of the Pennsylvania Dutch pavilion at the 1990 World's Fair. And there's a smell that teases me, unidentifiable, because everytime I sniff in the air after it, it's gone.

We're not too busy yet; people do their heavy buying in the afternoon. Even so, there are almost always great presses of people ringing the counters. Just looking. We're supposed to keep an eye out for shoplifters, but there's a limit to how far I'll go. I mean I won't go chasing anybody out the door and down through the lores yelling, "Get back here!" like Debbie Sheetz did yesterday. Over a measly Hex Power T-shirt. If I catch somebody scooping up key rings by the dozens, maybe I'll say, "We break knuckles for less than that," or "Will you be eating those here?" That's usually enough. If it isn't, tough brisket, Bittner!

A trio of related females, three generations worth, inch back through the stalled multitudes to where I'm leaning against the rear wall looking vigilant if not industrious. You know the connection right away because of the unmistakable pinch in the middle-aged woman's face. It's the pressed ham, a/k/a the sandwich look. (This is the single trait that Mom and I share: We see people as edibles. She'll say, "Does Dr. Meemish bring anything to mind?" and I'll say, "Easy, he's a broccoli." "Well, possibly," she'll answer. "More like a kohlrabi, don't you think? Same family though.") Poor woman's getting it from both ends, and in this heat. There's the little girl's greed coming at her and Grandma's nonstop piping in her ears.

Over the kid's whining for more, the woman says, "Just this. No bag. She'll put it right on," and hands me a card holding a bracelet with a single hex symbol in the center—raindrops for fertility. Who am I to argue?

The kid reaches out and strokes my long gingham skirt. "Where do *you* live, lady?" she singsongs.

"Why, dear," replies Grandma, "this is her little village. She lives right here."

"Oh, Mother," sighs Pressed Ham, "nobody *lives* here." She starts steering them none too gently by the elbows back out to the center aisle. The old woman keeps twisting a waxy white bird-face around and pecks at me with feisty little sparrow eyes.

Sure, lady, I get up in the morning and go to the teeny-weeny school, hit the teeny-weeny church on Sunday. I see myself as a tiny Alice skipping over the scaled-down cobblestone walks, leaping the low fences. Next week our entire "little village" will be stacked neatly in cartons and stored in Henninger's barn—a portable Brigadoon. I make a note to tell Caff; he's always been a sucker for muddled old ladies.

Finally Bittner holds up his hand and waves me out on break; he brings Debbie over from jams and jellies. Nuts to you, Caff! I go to the stand next to his where they squeeze real orange juice on the premises. And besides, as they say, I've got a friend in the business. Jimmy Lutz lays a Chumbo Chuicer on me and pretends to pick up some change. *He* understands the system. "Thanks, Lutz," I whisper. He nods like he's never seen me before.

There's not a breeze stirring in the whole county; I'd bet on it. The crowd swelling up from way down by the main gate gains strength from where I stand: straight back and slightly elevated. They look packed solid and on the move. I remember the history of the world and how waves of barbarians swept down from the north on a day just like today.

I notice the lady who bought the bracelet standing with her kid to the side of Caff's stand. Seeing me, the girl points and buries a grin in her mother's dress. The woman nods, smiling weakly and trying at the same time to pry the kid loose. Sipping my juice slowly, I move in closer and see that Grandma's doing business at the counter. She keeps turning to Middle and Little, saying "my treat, my treat," keeps looking back as if she's afraid they'll run away on her.

"Three fritters, three birch beers. Three-twenty," says Caff.

"Young man," she says, straining to lift her thin voice over the heads between her and the other two, "Don't you live here? Isn't this *too* your little village?" Hearing this, I crane to see Caff's face. Under the straw hat it's flushed—impatient and distracted. Not the hint of a smile. His eyes sweep the waiting customers. "Sure is, Ma'm," he says. "Three-twenty, please."

In her excitement, trying to juggle triumph and high finance, she can't seem to get to her coin purse and a pumping elbow tips a birch beer over onto the plate of sugared fritters. Caffrey calls to the back and one of those rotund types waddles up with a giant sponge.

"Three-twenty, Ma'm," Caffrey insists, but Pressed Ham has squeezed in next to her mother. Snapping Grandma's handbag shut, she tucks it under one arm and with the other leads the old lady out. Of the two surviving birch beers, one goes down Caffrey's gullet and one down the drain. And then it's business as usual while Granny shuffles off on a short leash and separates her grievances one pale strand at a time. Suddenly, my throat seizes up and I can't get the juice to go down.

Grabbing up my skirt I slip around the grass to the back of the tent where the ladies are peeling and slicing and mixing batter. I stick my face through the flap in the canvas and when Caff turns around to bark an order, I motion to him.

"Yeah?" he says when he comes back. He's got an eye on the counter and another on Little Chip who's emptying the cash box into a khaki bank bag.

I say, "Where should I meet you after work? You'll be done before me."

"I told you last night. At the square dance. Come up when you're done. That all?"

"I guess," I say, knowing that isn't all, not by a long shot. But the rest is just dust in my nostrils and a tightness across my brain.

"Chip says heavy on the peppers, light on the sausage," Caffrey tells the ladies in low tones. Then it's back to the customers with his darling-little-Dutch-boy bit. *"Kunst du micka fonga,"* he says. It's the only thing we know in Pennsylvania Dutch. It means "Can you catch flies?" Without a pause he answers himself: *"Ya, wonn sie hucka bleiva":* "Yes, if they sit still." But he makes it sound like *Hello, you terrific people, how 'bout a funnel cake?*

For a while I stand leaning into the shade of the tent, one hand clutching a support pole. It's like I'm needed here to hold the place up and everything depends on me not letting go. *Hang in here and keep watch.* I feel semi-attached, indispensible. But Bittner will be bumming big by now.

I'm about to head back when I see Little Chip take some bills out of the khaki bag and tuck them into Caffrey's back pocket as he stands bent over the cash box. One arm is around Caff's shoulder, his cigar-punched grin in his face. Maybe he speaks and maybe he doesn't but I hear him whisper: *Kid, I told you I'd make you a star.*

Afternoons around here drag on forever. By three the air has tentacles that won't let go. I'm socked in here with throngs of short-tempered, tormented folks still doggedly toiling after Family Fun. They carry huge tole decorated milk cans; their children have puffy red faces under two-dollar sunbonnets and hot black "Amish" hats. Their eyes are glassy, aimless. In them I see reflected my own stupid stare and there's one dull flat moment of a shapeless, nameless thing. Like shame. Like sorrow. But these things pass and now they start to grumble about the prices, demand impossible items. Do we have Latvian hex signs? Why aren't there more restrooms? Little wooden shoes? (How many times do I have to tell them that the Dutch are not Dutch as in Holland but Dutch as in Germany: Deutschland Dutch. And we don't have "little windmills" either.)

Just as the crowd starts to thin and Bittner settles down some, pulls in his long, theft-detecting neck, I notice the

back of a familiar pink sundress up by Dolls and Toys:
It's me. I mean it's my dress. The person in it is Mom.
She nutzes around the Raggedys for a while, then moves
on, faking an interest in Debbie's "country packed" apple butter, even buys a jar. She stops at Hex Signs and
bends Mrs. Gaugler's ear. Mom's meltingness—those soft
spreading edges—are too much on a hot day. Mrs.
Gaugler nods and looks faint.

"What are you doing?" I call to her when she gets
within earshot. As if I didn't know.

"Oh, I want to stop up at the quilt place."

"You did that yesterday."

"There's one I'd like to take another look at."

Mom doesn't lie, so I'm sure she'll go up and maybe
buy a freakin' quilt to make it true. But she's really here
for us, because we're here. She hands me a thermos of
lemonade; she's got another, presumably for Caff, who's
up to his elbows in the stuff already. Her eyes are
brimming with her great ungovernable liking for us.
God, she'll probably stand around all day soaking us in.
"Mom," I say, "Bittner doesn't like for us to socialize on
the job."

"You just go about your business." But pretty soon
she's clearing her throat and pointing with her eyes.
Across the aisle there's this lady with a giant geyser of
frosted hair spouting from the top of her head: obviously a pineapple.

"It's a fruit," she says.

"Ummmmm—a papaya?"

"I was thinking more a pineapple," she says, openly
disappointed.

"Yeah, well." I can be perverse.

I handle a couple of sales and when I look for her, she's over with Caff. In seconds she's back with a birch beer and her thoughtful, sherbet face.

"Caff bought me a drink," she says in a kind of wrung-out voice. "He's quite the little dynamo. But when did he get so . . . so . . . ?"

But I don't know what to call it either, so I can't finish her sentence until I look across the way at the burr of commercial energy that is my brother.

"So fried-fishy, Mom?"

"Uh-huh, that's it," she says.

I have to laugh. "Get going, Lydia Pinkham," I say. "Before all the quilts are gone."

I have the feeling that she leaves the building one molecule at a time, and it seems her slow pink misgivings leave a stain behind in the stale air. I keep thinking she's still hanging around, like a ghost or something.

Bittner hates to see "big bites out of the product line," so I take advantage of a brief lull to restock my pyramid. Things look a little calmer over at Caff's too. Just a man and his kid sharing a funnel cake under the striped awning. Behind the first row of deep-fryers, behind a lady dipping into the fat, hang the eyes of Little Chip. They are aimed at Caffrey's undefended back. (*Remember, Caff, how you took the go-cart right off the wall and into the woods and all that time the brittle stalk had been waiting in the leaves. We pulled it out like an arrow. You were dead or dying and all life came down to that sudden wound, the bold and blood-dark hole under your skinny white shoulder blades.*) Little Chip draws on his cigar and lets the smoke out slowly. I'm too far away, but I know he's smiling: *Kid, oh, kid, oh, you kid.*

When Bittner comes by, I can't look at his loose turkey throat or the patchy pink skin of his face. My stomach feels horribly iffy. It's the heat and the nearness of
Bittner; it's that odor coming and going, filling my head
or my nose. I'm not sure which. But it's stronger, and
now it has a name: It's the smell of ground cornmeal
mixed with the wood of wormy caskets.

Bittner is heading down the other way. I watch him
slip out the far entrance. "Hey," I yell. "Hey!" and gesture wildly in the opposite direction. And then I am off
the ground. "Bring that back!" I shout. I've got baskets
of words to toss along the way. "Stop that thief!" as I
point far ahead into the lazy afternoon crowd ambling
over the shadeless grounds. "Get back here!" I cry, and
on I run past the little church and the little school and
up through the lores and right by the gallows where
they're hanging Anna Metz, the baby slayer, for the two-
hundredth time. I even take a shortcut across the tin-
smith's corner and out behind the candlemaker's fires.
I stop shouting to hear the blood thump in my head. I
slow down and let my skirt drag. In April our orchard
sheds apple-blossom snow and Dad is in the hospital.
The petals float around my face. The air is full of spring
and hopelessness. Something, the sound I guess, makes
me look up and there's my brother stretched out on the
high dive above the empty white swimming pool. Caffrey alone and oblivious; Caffrey whistling and war-
bling and twittering in the soft evening air; Caffrey
ringed in the circle of white pines, the treetops trembling, full of breeze and the tiny disturbances of a mil-
lion flittering birds, the pines bending over him, the
birds returning his song. I think I am seeing a miracle.

* * *

In the barn the quilts are doubled over railings set into cement display tiers that rise up either side of the building. No problem to slip into the skinny tent formed by a king-size Star of Bethlehem. I sit motionless, hugging my knees: a weevil curled in the heart of this unfamiliar country. When I spot her, I'm not even sure. She's running back and forth between a tulip appliqué and a log cabin. She's standing around looking silly. Don't I have a dress like that? Doesn't the room look too big for her? Lydia Pinkham? I make up my mind if she starts plucking out her hair, I'll believe her. When she wanders by, I'll come out and see if she knows who I am.

In the Surprise of Life

This is a story of Christmas past and of a grandmother; yet there is Lilly wilting in the wash of now;
Lilly barefoot by the Lehigh River. Deepest, thickest
summer, the river's listless groping over stones, sky damp
and colorless as a cough. Her husband's passion is the
soft clay bank. Again and again his spade makes careful vertical incisions; the soil slices off like fudge.

These banks are lavishly nuggeted with Leni-Lenape
artifacts. Other weekends his toil was rewarded early,
easily. Today the earth itself is a stony squaw, sullen with
secrets, yielding nothing. Lilly's efforts are all *against*
mud, keeping her knees clean and her toddling daughter out of the soggy riverbed. At thirty-seven she is an
old mother; this is hard work. The sagging air, the
rhythmic scrape of his tool, swallows sweeping in to sip.
She thinks of fern beds, of putting greens, of shade, of
sleep. . . . Suddenly, what? A hardly remarkable stir?
a deeper stillness? Whatever its shape, the moment is
marked; it is hers. She goes to her husband, thrusts out
the child. "One second," she says. He hands her the
spade. With hardly a pause she chooses her spot and
sinks the shovel deep. One confident cut; moist clay curls
stiffly away, crumbles. The psychic nudge does nothing
to tame the thrill of what she sees. Not just an arrow-
head but a splendid find, a polished jasper paintpot,

partly uncovered: a timid eye blinking the scree of centuries.

And stooping to retrieve one muddy treasure, she discovers another, as if the latter had dropped like a rock from her bent head. Something she had not thought about in years. An event can be like that: humble in the happening, meekly biding a brown oblivion in the wrack and scrap of time; memories working in the lapse like the virtuous dead aching to be canonized.

Lilly McShea is in seventh grade. Tall and toothy, knobby with popping bones. Everybody's case in point of the Three Poors—attitude, posture, Palmer Method. Her life reads like an inventory of things misplaced and lost: records, radios, homework, lunch money. Her best friend, Gretchen Loobie, because she borrowed her slambook and left it in the ladies' room in the uptown Rialto. A Tuesday's child despite Mrs. McShea's sputtering insistence that Lilly was born on a Friday night, "easy as throwing up supper."

Her dumbness and disadvantage are issues she eagerly supports in hope of kindly avuncular rebuttal, rarely forthcoming. And the proofs, in any case, leave little room for debate: (1) the rigid corps of D's on her last report card; (2) down at the Teen Canteen only one person has ever asked her to dance—a stubbly geezer reeking of camphor who was later led cursing back to the Lutheran Home; (3) the regular chalk-eraser drubbings from Sister Emory which keep her hair prematurely, if lopsidedly, gray; (4) she killed a dracaena once, as best as she can figure, by breathing on it.

They say she "writes well," but what is that when every

paper is at the mercy of the school-issue pen, which routinely up and punctuates her best sentence with a monstrous blob of midnight-blue slobber: *this*, for pity's sake, is *not* her fault. Her chin describes an oscillating arc between bashful and belligerent. A blushing brat. One of those hell-bent, but-but-butting teacher-baiters about whom lurks the mushroom cloud of an endless classroom groan.

Her "folks" are a decent, soft-spoken sort, holding everything—mortgage, conviction, outrage—as tenants in common. ("We like our peace and quiet, our coffee black. We *loathe* shirkers!") Lilly has refashioned their faces into pliant molds of matched dismay. Unstable stares she fears will distort in the hardening, twist to grimace or bunch in irreversible disgust.

In the kitchen, Mrs. McShea is filling miniature pie shells she's cut out with Coke-bottle bottoms. Lilly understands these are for canasta club, and as the filling happens to be creamed peas, it's just as well. "Can I have one?" she pipes anyhow. Just to see her mother's supple *come-now* face, hear her sigh. Hear her say, "Have a banana." The flatness of the woman's voice makes Lilly blurt, "How the heck can I help it some jerk steals one freakin sneaker. Just tell me, how's that *my* fault?"

A blast of bitter air rattles the cupboards. The door slams shut, appears to shove Muzza into the kitchen. She's wearing a karakul coat, her plaid babushka gabled high over a crown of iron-gray braids. Two cold red bunions poke through holes in outsized brown corduroy Keds. On her lapel, a plastic Rudolph pin, the face painted mean as a mink's. Despite the temperature and Mr. McShea's willingness to "fetch" her, she has come stubbornly on foot from Bantell Street, down through the steep, rooty woods, down the Easy Grade, across Estey, and up, up, up their own merciless Hill Street. She gathers Lilly close against her cold coat, the smell of cold clenched deep in her fur.

"Vell, Mutska," she says. Her Ajax smile, wire glasses low on a plunging nose. "You ready paint town red with *starababba?*"

The suspicion that she is too old to go tooting around town with a funny-tongued grandmother is mixed with the laggardly lure of the marked trail. Known hazards. Let Muzza do the talking, drag along like something dredged; hard to lose a gym shoe on Main Street. "I don't care," she says, shrugging.

Now Muzza points to the dough scraps left on the rolling board. "Anna," she admonishes, "don't trow way. Ve come back. I roll up with little cinnamon, sugar, bake. Last dough good as first."

"See that dirty skillet on the stove, Mother," says Mrs. McShea, being droll. "Shall I save it so you can make soup?"

"That depend what you fry. Lamb chop? Kielbasa? I put little water, garlic, salt, pepper—"

"Out of my kitchen, you two greiners. Go, go." Laughing, she shoos them with her floury apron. "And don't bring home any chicken feet or pig's knuckles."

Lilly grabs her pea jacket, her green toboggan cap, and they leave, two rangy ladies tilting stiffly downhill to the Estey Street trolley stop.

The face of downtown Christmas has already dulled to a frazzled, shopworn sorriness. Holly collars around the light stanchions have a lusterless, brittle look. The beards of sidewalk Santas are ashy, their suits mustard-stained and dingy. In a mill town the skies rain grime regardless of season.

First the errands: the light bill, the coal company, the bank. They cut over to Market Street, dawdle in front of Jurcic's Funeral Home, where Muzza studies the somber black-and-white signboard. If the deceased happens to be Slovenian or even close—Croatian, Polish, Slovak—she will press upon Lilly a clean handkerchief and the two of them go trundling in. AMIDIO J. VIZZINI, Lilly reads with relief, even though the muted pleasures of past occasions—when these affairs limned the dominant social motif of her childhood—still linger. The pinkened gladiola air, priests and nuns nodding like limp black flowers, the foreign syllables—thickly sibilant—compressed to a rich, mysterious, gummy hum. In a way, she had grown up in this house, had in fact grown tall if a little spindly around the procession of gunmetal-gray coffins, the biers of perfect—oh, better than perfect—strangers. And Muzza holding the baffled widow's hand; Muzza suddenly, coruscatingly beautiful, transfigured with tears. Nobody ever said, *Who are you? What do you want with our grief?*

On then to Bender's Yard Goods, where they settle on a celery wool for Lilly's Christmas dress. "Don't make it too long," she says. The whisper of conspiracy is the sound that hushes their history—too many schemes to count, this one against Mrs. McShea and the nuns who would hold '58 hemlines to mid-calf. In compliance with Lilly's directives, Muzza has been sneaking up her skirts a half-inch at a time. "You bet," Muzza says now. "American way. Short and sweet." She cocks her head, eyes beguiled. "Short and sweet, short and sweet," she intones deliciously, her tongue on the words tasting and zestful. She rocks back on her heels, sways, dips, flutters her meager chest. The pulling surf of girlish, self-conscious laughter. "Don't get started," Lilly chides, "or you'll pee your Pechglos."

At the Rexall, Muzza picks up a bottle of Father John's tonic, a tin of talc. While they wait to pay, Lilly slips a roll of Tums off the rack and into her pocket, believes, by some private logic, the store has invited this: something about the sourness of life, something about the way the wan little clerk answers Muzza's sportive friendliness with a waspish, superior reserve. Muzza draws two singles from her small, black, principled coin purse. The potato-digging hand, coarsened and stained, her middle finger broken in one of those willful treks down from Bantell Street, permanently crooked like a comma; next to it, the diamond Tata bought her at seventy, when he understood finally that he was dying. Lilly's clear claim on the Tums fuzzes. In plain view of the priggish clerk, she pops them back on the counter; she meets his eyes coldly, smartly: a wordless challenge between equals.

Later, on Main Street, Muzza notices the green toboggan cap is missing. Lilly punishes her skull with both fists. "Oh, spit!" Then: "Somebody must have hooked it. Some grubby Front Street kid, no doubt." Muzza pinches her cheek. "You big little palooka," she says with such effortless delight that Lilly is tempted to question the wrong in her wrongheadedness—indeed, to credit herself with some rare elusive charm.

"Anyhow, I hate ugly ting," Muzza is saying. "Look

like Ravnik peasant hat. Ve go over Edelman Brothers, get something nice color. Maybe red. Maybe sexy as heck."

It's no secret that Muzza is soft on American. She prefers the fluff of Wonder Bread to her own hefty loaves. She loves and loves to say Snickers bars and Dairy Queen, soda jerks and Snooky Lanson. Shamelessly she mines conversations for new clichés and snappy phrases; takes them home, drills till they're perfect, polished as her kettles. Eventually she tries them out in public, sometimes ruinously. At Tata's wake, when Father Navenshek finished his sour-cream strukla, yawned and looked at his watch, Muzza leaned over, her tone deeply solicitous. "Fadder," she said, "vot time you must blow dis joint?"

After buying the cap—a soft confection of raspberry angora that matches nothing Lilly has ever owned—they go over to Foodfare for the *potitsa* ingredients. What was once the main event of a gleeful spree is now just another errand. But early joys have a way of embering down, burning low, and the old woman's renewed ebullience catches in Lilly, fans small pockets of pale, watched fires. Their selection is careful. "Peticular," says Muzza. They choose the walnuts one at a time, examine the color of the honey. "Your eggs nice and fresh?" Muzza asks the stockboy. He nods minutely. "You better slap them," she cracks. She always says this, in just this genial, enjoying way, and yet now Lilly sways with the shock of sudden embarrassment. She bucks off with the cart, lurching far ahead of Muzza, past the dairy case and around the corner. Up the next aisle, briskly. As if she is no stranger to purposeful hustle, a competent young woman entrusted with the family food shopping. As if she is a *real* person. At the flour section she stops and guiltily waits for Muzza, but what overtakes her first are simple hunger pangs fed with irrepressible visions of *potitsas* puffing and crusting in Muzza's oven. To consider now the rich spirals of nutcrumbly filling would be unbearable. For each of her three daughters' families Muzza will make one great loaf, rolled and plumply coiled, bigger than a bread box. By Christmas Eve they will be snugly in hand, but not until after Mass the next day will anyone dare do more than snitch a pinch of loose crust or a fleshy gouge from the bottom. Her stomach grumblings, she understands, betoken a ritual rightness: In the excitement of these jaunts, they have always neglected to eat, and very soon anyhow Muzza's purse will be flat as Lilly's pocket, empty as her heart.

That night Muzza stays over at Hill Street. For want of a spare room, Muzza always sleeps with Lilly in her pineapple poster bed. It used to be she would implore Muzza to spend the night, each time prompting an unvarying exchange. Muzza: "What crazy person like sleep with skinny old hunky lady?" Lilly: "Skinny hunky kid." Muzza: "How you can be hunky kid with such name like McShea?" Lately, though, the practice seems sadly tarnished, tacky as downtown Christmas. Like undershirts or drinking buttermilk (which she and Muzza did, by the gallon, in the stuporous summers, in the Bantell Street kitchen).

Nor is she much disposed any more to badger the old woman for "stories." Over the years her rapt enchantment has goaded Muzza to outrageous perjuries, the same old-country sagas reworked, enlarged, enlivened with late-night liberties and silliness, so that, in the end, preposterousness was its own fulfillment. Far into the night the bed rocked with laughter (Muzza has a high unruly giggle somehow connected directly to her bladder). And Mrs. McShea would have to come in and, as if they were a couple of slumber-party cutups, whimperingly plead her need for sleep. *"Starababba!"* Muzza would whisper, when her daughter was gone. "Old woman."

More recently, when a tale is told, the teller is likely to be Lilly. And the practice is inexcusable, a dark and shameful breach of a firm family taboo: *Don't tell Muzza. She'll fret herself to death.* Inside, her grandmother is all melt, oceans of ready sympathy that can be tapped like a vat. For months now, under cover of night, Lilly has been slipping her worries, feeding her woes. Whispering sadness into her heart like a slow poison. Every lump and bump and blister, the mad dog, the lurking maniac, a sliver of glass Muzza will understand is wending a deadly course from Lilly's finger to her heart. She's addicted to Muzza's tears, floats blankly in their lenient broth as something yet to be and loath to be born.

Now she draws a breath before launching a barrage of recent wretchedness. Indifferent young men, abandonments and betrayals, injustices and mortifications. Spiteful Gretchen Loobie. "I'm cursed," she snivels. "Jinxed forever." And seeing that Muzza's grief has not yet ripened in her eyes, she scrambles to the crest of the worst she can think of. "I have nothing to live for," she says. "How long do I have?"

"Vot how long? Vot you mean?"

"How long till the glass zaps my heart? It would truly be a blessing," she says, borrowing the words, the pious tone from the widows of Jurcic's.

In the beginning Muzza's weeping is soundless, perceptible only as luminosity of darkness, the night billowing silkily around them. Then, "How-you-can-say-such-ting?" Each word strangled, each word the bitter core of a separate sob. Bony hands dig into Lilly's arm. The shuddering mattress. Then long, raking, ragged gasps. They lie side by side on their backs; tears pour from Muzza's face onto Lilly's pillow. No bottom to this welling. What has she started? Panicked imaginings of tears like blood. How many pints can a person lose? Visions of Muzza lying dry and cheekless as an apple doll. In the end Muzza turns to the wall, hoards her grief, baffles it the way proud people hide pain from the puncher. Soft lobs of lament, private, estranged, and Lilly comes frightened across the distance, awkward with retraction, sodden with remorse. "Don't mind me, Muzza. Just one of my stupid moods." She drapes herself over Muzza's shoulders, tries to suspend an upside-down grin in front of her face: "Look, I'm smiling." And that having little effect, she draws back and says, "Maybe I'd get really happy if you'd tell me . . . tell me about the time you pulled the plug on your daddy's nasty wine." "No!" Muzza says, sharply.

Long minutes pass; time running for dignity, smoothing itself like a rumpled apron. Muzza dabbing her eyes with a soft white sleeve. "I vill tell you instead sad story, terrible story." She pauses, sniffs. "First Christmas your Tata and I are marry, he come home from number two mine, eat and go to bed. Always this

his habit for he must get up again at four. It is lovely silent night, holy night. Snow is falling deep on street. I go over visit my friend Mrs. Svoboda. Ve talk little, eat *sganzas*. I have small glass gooseberry wine. Ven I come home it is late, maybe half past hour of nine. I am careful not to wake him. Take off shoes, put on nice lawn nightgown. Suddenly he sit up in bed, eyes big like gold piece. I see hate, murder. I see my skinny neck snap like chicken's. Next ting he holler, "Now I got you, *hoodich*. You svine. By holy Rochus, now you vill pay." Tank God I am near door. I run so fast like never in life. Down dark back steps. Out on street. Two block I run with nekkid feet and pretty nightgown back to house of Mrs. Svoboda." She pauses significantly. Her next words spew breathy reprimand: "How you like such crazy mix-up Christmas? How *you* like, Mutska?"

Her words, swirling, fragile as snowflakes, deliquesce into darkness. Gone, gone. Tata, too. Given to Lilly *after* the rage, in the season of his shy, venturing tenderness. A man with fruit trees and a thousand gimmicks for giving quarters. Gone, seamlessly as the words. She tries to envision Muzza, at nineteen or twenty, a graceful wraith haunting the bleary street, but sees only this bony old woman in desperate, squawking flight, the big yellow-bunioned feet slapping the blameless snow. The adult solemnity in which she and Muzza lie nodding, sage as county home pensioners, dissolves too, and the sounds that rip from her are not unlike the yips of a terrier.

"What he tink?" Muzza says now. "I am big Welsh crew boss?" Her chest starts to heave and within seconds they are choking, rocking, gasping like bad motors, laughing and crying, catching back in tandem only long enough to listen for suffering footsteps down the long hall.

Late on the afternoon of Christmas Eve, Muzza comes stomping in out of the weather. She is empty-handed. "I bring bad news," she reports grimly. "It is *potitsa*." They stare at her, incredulous; the woman is immune to culinary failure. "Of course," she says, "*potitsa* is fine, like always." She spreads the fingers of her left hand. In the middle of Tata's ring is a raw, shocking hole where the stone had been and the sight makes them cry out as if pinched. "Only ting," she says, "*potitsa* have new ingredient this year. I only notice when loaves are on table to cool."

They are talking diamonds, talking Tata, yet nobody bothers to suggest the obvious: that any halfway reasonable person would have panicked and clawed those breads to shreds. But Muzza lives by the law of use, in her heart and on her table, an exalted place for leftovers. What curse, what hellish thing would rise from the rubble of three plundered *potitsas*? "So," she is saying. "I tink I have figger out vot to do. Everybody come up Bantell Street after church, eat *potitsa* under nose of cook, so I can keep eye on operation."

Muzza's table has but one extra leaf, and the relatives gathered around it form a rictus as of crowded, uneven teeth. They appear uneasy and, at the same time, tautly expectant, as if they'd been herded here to witness some startling revelation. Lilly finds it wonderfully new and comical. Her hefty aunts and their strapping steelworker husbands, the male cousins—hellions all three—held to a tea-party daintiness. The nibbling bites, the thoughtful, dubious chewing. Muzza slices the bread herself into thin volumes like poetry. Then she sits back, nodding around the table, eyes widening with each committed chomp, shuddering as each Adam's apple signals a fully executed swallow. The stillness swells, the air as densely sacrosanct as just before Communion. But solemnity sits uneasy on Muzza's face, the slack muscles struggling to uphold the look of an elder presiding gravely. When she catches Lilly's eye, she comes apart like a slow-ripping seam, giggles into her hands. Her shoulders shake; her glasses bump down her nose. Her eyes brim and when her mouth molds a surprised O, Lilly knows she's wet her pants.

The family laughs, but tightly, in the provisional manner of people trapped in someone else's hilarity. They take up a sparse chatter. "Don't the Chinese or somebody make traitors swallow diamonds?" "Not at today's prices, Alice," says Mrs. McShea. "You're thinking of glass," somebody else offers. "Ground glass— shreds your innards."

It is not, nor will it turn out to be a white Christmas, but Lilly senses the moment the same way that late, late at night you know it's begun to snow: a yielding thing. A subtle shift, as if the weather is inside you. Her heart quickens; her cheeks warm. Hands trembling, she breaks her slice in two. The stone is cool, restrained, smugly coddled in a plump yellow raisin. It clings for an instant, then drops ringingly onto her plate, seems to come awake in a tantrum of polychromatic sparkle, punching back the bold hues of Muzza's hanging lamp. Like a tiny, somewhat feisty fallen star. Everybody cheers and

applauds. In the glow of her own starshine Lilly grins
brazenly. She reels with the sudden weightlessness of
someone plucked in the nick of time from certain catastrophe. Someone favored by heaven. Is it possible she
is after all, rather splendid? A genuine benefactor? And
reshaping her face along more modest lines, she lifts
the stone from the crumbs and places it in Muzza's mud-
yellowed palm.

The grandmother stands. Squared shoulders. The face
of a matriarch but Lilly sees a rakish spark in the slanted
Yugoslav eyes. "I have many," she says, "how you say—
people vot live after me. Only one ring. Today I decide
finder keeper. Ven I kick bucket"—and a protesting
pulse trembles the room—"ven time come," she says
firmly, "Tata's diamond go to Lilly. Fair is fair."

Late afternoon. Drawn shades squeeze fiery wands of
light across the bed where the child naps between her
parents. Ceiling vents breathe jets of cooling air. A
blissful dimness, the river afternoon lingering in the
smell of sun and mud and sweat, swaddling them damp-
ly in fatigue and a dreamy kind of contentment. On the
dresser sits the jasper paintpot: the polished fact of their
good fortune. In Lilly's hand the ring, retrieved from
its ancient cotton, for she has been telling the story,
telling her husband as he drowsily nods; telling it mostly
for her own amazement. "Know what I think?" she says
now, excitedly. The rise in her voice flutters his eyelids.
"Muzza was a practical sort," she says. "Every Christmas she got me what I needed most."

"You needed a diamond?" he says.

"That low-down dreadful year, what I needed most was luck."

Yawning, he says, "Love? Did you say love?"

"Well, that too. Maybe luck needs love to recognize itself. But what I'm trying to say: It never dawned on me till now—why, I'd lay odds that *potitsa* was rigged from start to finish. Like a prisoner's cake, you know. Like Tata's quarters turning up in socks."

His lips vibrate softly. *Hmmmmmmmmm, Hmmmmmmmmm.* His breath evens out and it doesn't really matter that nobody hears her words go by easy as water over stones. She'd never told him, she says, touching the girl's cheek, that after fourteen years of childlessness, she had felt the fusion of their cells in her belly, a soft pop like thread breaking as she made the bed that day. She'd touched the spot. "I knew. I knew," she whispers.

And then what she doesn't speak but merely thinks: that the time came when Muzza began to prefer her native expressions, hunger for black breads and mushrooms from the Ravnik woods. Gift chocolates sat pat, unoffered on her lap, hoarded like that long-ago grief, and her eyes traveled imperturbably past worries. And the family met Muzza's daily diminution with baffled panic, tried and found they lacked her gift for inventive tenderness; and that, worse, nobody knew how to make the foods—the *potitsas*, the *struklas*, the *sganzas*— she craved even when full. And one night, long after Lilly married, her sleep had opened like an awed eye upon the moment of Muzza's death; and the grief, too, was open and outward, translucent as the pink pulsant

213

mystery of Jurcic's Funeral Home. When the phone rang
she picked it up and said, "I know," and began a lifetime of missing her.

And something even more tenuous, softer than
thought. A view perhaps from the soul—of what is unknown to her and yet known, here and yet gone; of the
way she lives now in the surprise of life, like a tiny miner
masquerading in street clothes; of all the things that
encapsule things and those still others and on to the
smallest, most infinitesimal amazement; of the meanness and rage that also yield; but mostly, of all that is
good and bright and sometimes funny locked in the
obdurate mud, the stern, pretending faces.

And in *her*? Deep, deep, deeper than she could ever
reach or explain, a persisting expectant thing, warm like
love, sharp like joy—often unreasoned and perfectly
unprovoked—embedded there, as it were, in the heart.
As if she had indeed not found but swallowed that diamond, and it burned, burned, burned but had hardly
harmed her.

Her husband stirs, speaks thickly out of his torpor.
She leans her ear to his mouth. "I believe you," he says,
and sleeps.

ABOUT THE AUTHOR

Sharon Sheehe Stark is married and has two children. She lives in Lenhartsville, Pennsylvania.